A Drea

By Edward John Moreton Drax Plunkett Dunsany

Foreword by James Portnow
Edited by Jac Mindelan

Last Chance Books
Seattle, WA

The First Dreamer

I found myself in Carcassone...

For those of you who have not read this book before: there is a story here, as you turn these pages, called Carcassone; a story of an endless search, a quest with no conclusion or reward. When I first read the story I showed it to those around me; to friends, to family. They found it sad and wistful, but I found something different in it. I found it to be a story of the greatest hope, because it was a story of not giving up long, long after hope was gone. To some it was a story of futility, but to me it was a story of refusing to abandon the thing you know you must do, even if you realize that it may be futile. It was a story of striving, and striving was the point: not the path, the plot, or the means to an end.

It's a story I call to mind whenever my days are too heavy, whenever the struggle is too much, whenever it would be easier to just accept the world as it is rather than as it should be.

But each person finds something different in Dunsany, which is why I wanted to help bring this edition to life. Because Dunsany's work has touched everyone from Robert E. Howard to H. P. Lovecraft, Arthur C. Clarke to

Jorge Luis Borges, Gene Wolfe to Tolkien, Michel Moorcock to Ursula K. Le Guin, David Eddings to Peter Beagle, even Guillermo Del Toro and Neil Gaiman.

Dunsany gave us the words "Mountains of Madness" and caused Lovecraft to once lament that he himself could only mimic Poe or Dunsany but could never discover what it meant to write like Lovecraft. He was one of Robert Howard's favorite poets. He and Clarke wrote a whole book of letters to one another, and Borges introduced him to the Spanish speaking world. The first time Tolkien brought in an outsider to look at a manuscript of the Silmarillion he handed them a copy of Dunsany's Book of Wonder first. Ursula K. Le Guin jokingly warned young writers that the biggest fantasy novelist's trap was being a tourist in Elfland rather than living in it. David Eddings, on the other hand, recommended that any young writer of fantasy check Dunsany out. And of course Neil Gaiman's never been shy about the impact that Dunsany had on him.

So why have we forgotten him? Why do names like H.G. Wells and Jules Verne live in our collective memory while Dunsany, father of fantasy, has been largely forgotten? Is it because Dunsany is difficult to read? His prose are archaic in the way only a noble son of 19th century Ireland's can be. His sentences move at a pace no longer present in our telecommuting, 24-hour news, internet age.

And that's certainly part of it; no publisher wants to re-print work that they think is too difficult for their audience to read.

They are of course wrong. To an audience who eats up Tolkien and Bradbury and Lovecraft, Dunsany is an adjustment but not a challenge.

So why did we lose track of Dunsany? Was it because his later work largely wasn't fantasy? Was it because fantasy itself doesn't have the sort of continuous thread that you can tie between works of science fiction? Because there's 30 years between The King of Elfland's Daughter and the first printing of Lord of the Rings, and because in between things look a lot more like Conan the Barbarian?

Yes, I think there's that too, but most of all I think it is the tenor of his work. Fantasy is supposed to be an escape where swords are swung, spells are cast and the shining knight gets the girl... or at least, that's what the vast majority of what has been published in the genre since the 70s would try to tell you.

Dunsany is not that. There is a beautiful melancholy to Dunsany a sorrow that finds joy in being able to see the beauty of sorrow, a joy made the more poignant by the fact that it will not last. Dunsany is not dour or grimdark like much of the work today that tries to buck the weight of Tolkien on the genre. Rather Dunsany's works are in-fused with a verve, a love of life, even at times an impish humor, but they also hold in them a feeling of something slipping away, of a fond memory, of loss that you can only smile at because it means you once had. And it is this, this feeling, that I think has kept publishers from reprinting his works. I think many publishers really do look at the fantasy audience and think we only want an escape, that unless things can be described with words like 'operatic', 'badass' or 'cool' we do not want them.

This too is false.

It has been since the genre began. Dunsany is the father of fantasy. While there were a few other pieces that we might today consider part of the genre that pre-dated his writing, Dunsany's works were the first to reach a mass audience, he was the first author to sustain a fantasy world in work after work, and perhaps most importantly, he was the first fantasy author to create a mythos.

All world building in literature, all sprawling realms with heroes and gods and history that you feel like you know, owe him a debt. When he created Pegāna, he brought together his love of the style he found in the King James Bible, his wonder at the world of the Greek Gods and his fascination with the fantastic imagery of Poe and did something that no one else had done before: he created a whole new mythology.

He created this mythology not because he thought it was real or because he wanted to found a new system of worship. He created it because he wanted to tell stories,

stories that couldn't necessarily be told in the world we live in. This was truly new.

Fantasy couldn't exist without that first step. That realization that we can build a world of the mind. That we can people it with creatures and civilizations and gods just as real to us as our own...all the while knowing it's unreal. And that's what Dunsany gave us.

Fantasy is not simply an escape. It is not simply a genre for those who don't want to do the work of reading "real" books. Fantasy can bring us to other worlds and help us better understand our own lives. Fantasy doesn't have to live only on the poles of swords and sorcery and the grimmest of grimdark. We as an audience desire and are ready for so much more.

It is my hope that with this book we prove this in some small way. It is my hope too that some of you may find inspiration in these words and that perhaps one of these years I will be writing an intro to another Dunsany book and, as I'm penning the litany of people who have found something in his work, perhaps, just perhaps, I will get to add a new name. It is my hope I might add you.

JP

Then they drew their swords, and side by side went down into the forest, still seeking Carcassonne...

Table of Contents

I hope for this book that it may come into the hands of those that were kind to my others and that it may not disappoint them.

—Lord Dunsany

Poltarnees, Beholder of Ocean

Toldees, Mondath, Arizim, these are the Inner Lands, the lands whose sentinels upon their borders do not behold the sea. Beyond them to the east there lies a desert, for ever untroubled by man: all yellow it is, and spotted with shadows of stones, and Death is in it, like a leopard lying in the sun. To the south they are bounded by magic, to the west by a mountain, and to the north by the voice and anger of the Polar wind.[1] Like a great wall is the mountain to the west. It comes up out of the distance and goes down into the distance again, and it is named Poltarnees, Beholder of Ocean. To the northward red rocks, smooth and bare of soil, and without any speck of moss or herbage, slope up to the very lips of the Polar wind, and there is nothing else there by the noise of his anger. Very peaceful are the Inner Lands, and very fair are their cities, and there is no war among them, but quiet and ease. And they have no enemy but age, for thirst and fever lie sunning themselves out in the mid-desert, and never prowl

---

[1] "When people ask me about 'a book that changed my life,' one of the several hundred honest answers I can give them is A Dreamer's Tales... from the first sentence I was a goner." -Ursula K. Le Guin.

into the Inner Lands. And the ghouls and ghosts, whose highway is the night, are kept in the south by the boundary of magic. And very small are all their pleasant cities, and all men are known to one another therein, and bless one another by name as they meet in the streets. And they have a broad, green way in every city that comes in out of some vale or wood or downland,[2] and wanders in and out about the city between the houses and across the streets, and the people walk along it never at all, but every year at her appointed time Spring walks along it from the flowery lands, causing the anemone to bloom on the green way and all the early joys of hidden woods, or deep, secluded vales, or triumphant downlands, whose heads lift up so proudly, far up aloof from cities.[3]

Sometimes waggoners or shepherds walk along this way, they that have come into the city from over cloudy ridges, and the townsmen hinder them not, for there is a tread that troubleth the grass and a tread that troubleth it not, and each man in his own heart knoweth which tread he hath. And in the sunlit spaces of the weald and in the

---

[2] Downs and specifically Downlands are the chalky hills common to the British Isles. Its name comes from the Old Irish word dún. It's the same word JRR Tolkien will later use to describe the Barrow Downs in the Lord of the Rings.

[3] Upon reading this paragraph H.P. Lovecraft said it had "arrested me as with an electric shock and I had not read two pages before I became a Dunsany devotee for life."

wold's[4] dark places, afar from the music of cities and from the dance of the cities afar, they make there the music of the country places and dance the country dance. Amiable, near and friendly appears to these men the sun, and as he is genial to them and tends their younger vines, so they are kind to the little woodland things and any rumour of the fairies or old legend. And when the light of some little distant city makes a slight flush upon the edge of the sky, and the happy golden windows of the homesteads stare gleaming into the dark, then the old and holy figure of Romance, cloaked even to the face, comes down out of hilly woodlands and bids dark shadows to rise and dance, and sends the forest creatures forth to prowl, and lights in a moment in her bower of grass the little glowworm's lamp, and brings a hush down over the grey lands, and out of it rises faintly on far-off hills the voice of a lute. There are not in the world lands more prosperous and happy than Toldees, Mondath, Arizim.

From these three little kingdoms that are named the Inner Lands the young men stole constantly away. One by one they went, and no one knew why they went save that they had a longing to behold the Sea. Of this longing they spoke little, but a young man would become silent for a

---

[4] The Weald is an old English term for a woodland; Wold is a Germanic word (etymologically related to the word 'wild') referring to a piece of uncultivated land.

few days, and then, one morning very early, he would slip away and slowly climb Poltarnees' difficult slope, and having attained the top pass over and never return. A few stayed behind in the Inner Lands and became the old men, but none that had ever climbed Poltarnees from the very earliest times had ever come back again. Many had gone up Poltarnees sworn to return. Once a king sent all his courtiers, one by one, to report the mystery to him, and then went himself; none ever returned.

Now, it was the wont of the folk of the Inner Lands to worship rumours and legends of the Sea, and all that their prophets discovered of the Sea was writ in a sacred book, and with deep devotion on days of festival or mourning read in the temples by the priests. Now, all their temples lay open to the west, resting upon pillars, that the breeze from the Sea might enter them, and they lay open on pillars to the east that the breezes of the Sea might not be hindered by pass onward wherever the Sea list. And this is the legend that they had of the Sea, whom none in the Inner Lands had ever beholden. They say that the Sea is a river heading towards Hercules[5], and they say that he touches against the edge of the world, and that Poltarnees looks upon him. They say that all the worlds of heaven go

------

[5] This refers not to the ancient Greek mythological hero, but the constellation.

bobbing on this river and are swept down with the stream, and that Infinity is thick and furry with forests through which the river in his course sweeps on with all the worlds of heaven.[6]   Among the colossal trunks of those dark trees, the smallest fronds of whose branches are many nights, there walk the gods. And whenever its thirst, glowing in space like a great sun, comes upon the beast, the tiger of the gods creeps down to the river to drink. And the tiger of the gods drinks his fill loudly, whelming worlds the while, and the level of the river sinks between its banks ere the beast's thirst is quenched and ceases to glow like a sun. And many worlds thereby are heaped up dry and stranded, and the gods walk not among them evermore, because they are hard to their feet.[7]   These are the worlds that have no destiny, whose people know no god. And the river sweeps onwards ever. And the name of the River is Oriathon, but men call it Ocean. This is the Lower Faith of the Inner Lands. And there is a Higher Faith which is not told to all. Oriathon sweeps on through the forests of Infinity and all at once falls roaring over an Edge, whence

---

[6] The first half of the sentence refers to the vastness of the sea, where one might look out and not be able to tell where the sky ends and the water begins. The second half of the sentence refers to the ancientness of the sea: the forests in this case are a metaphor for all of the infinite places and continents the sea has flown through.
[7] This is a beautiful metaphor for the tides; the tiger of the gods drinks the river dry until the planets and constellations, or gods, are no longer reflected in the water; they are hard to their feet.

Time has long ago recalled his hours to fight in his war with the gods; and falls unlit by the flash of nights and days, with his flood unmeasured by miles, into the deeps of nothing.

Now as the centuries went by and the one way by which a man could climb Poltarnees became worn with feet, more and more men surmounted it, not to return. And still they knew not in the Inner Lands upon what mystery Poltarnees looked. For on a still day and windless, while men walked happily about their beautiful streets or tended flocks in the country, suddenly the west wind would bestir himself and come in from the Sea. And he would come cloaked and grey and mournful and carry to someone the hungry cry of the Sea calling out for bones of men. And he that heard it would move restlessly for some hours, and at last would rise suddenly, irresistibly up, setting his face to Poltarnees, and would say, as is the custom of those lands when men part briefly, "Till a man's heart remembereth," which means "Farewell for a while"; but those that loved him, seeing his eyes on Poltarnees, would answer sadly, "Till the gods forget," which means "Farewell."

Now the king of Arizim had a daughter who played with the wild wood flowers, and with the fountains in her father's court, and with the little blue heaven-birds that came to her doorway in the winter to shelter from the snow. And she was more beautiful than the wild wood

6

flowers, or than all the fountains in her father's court, or than the blue heaven-birds in their full winter plumage when they shelter from the snow. The old wise kings of Mondath and of Toldees saw her once as she went lightly down the little paths of her garden, and turning their gaze into the mists of thought, pondered the destiny of their Inner Lands. And they watched her closely by the stately flowers, and standing alone in the sunlight, and passing and repassing the strutting purple birds that the king's fowlers had brought from Asagéhon. When she was of the age of fifteen years the King of Mondath called a council of kings. And there met with him the kings of Toldees and Arizim. And the King of Mondath in his Council said:

"The call of the unappeased and hungry Sea (and at the word 'Sea' the three kings bowed their heads) lures every year out of our happy kingdoms more and more of our men, and still we know not the mystery of the Sea, and no devised oath has brought one man back. Now thy daughter, Arizim, is lovelier than the sunlight, and lovelier than those stately flowers of thine that stand so tall in her garden, and hath more grace and beauty than those strange birds that the venturous fowlers bring in creaking wagons out of Asagéhon, whose feathers are alternate purple and white. Now, he that shall love thy daughter, Hilnaric, whoever he shall be, is the man to climb Poltarnees and return, as none hath ever before, and tell us

7

upon what Poltarnees looks; for it may be that they daughter is more beautiful than the Sea."

Then from his Seat of Council arose the King of Arizim. He said: "I fear that thou hast spoken blasphemy against the Sea, and I have a dread that ill will come of it. Indeed I had not thought she was so fair. It is such a short while ago that she was quite a small child with her hair still unkempt and not yet attired in the manner of princesses, and she would go up into the wild woods unattended and come back with her robes unseemly and all torn, and would not take reproof with a humble spirit, but made grimaces even in my marble court all set about with fountains."

Then said the King of Toldees:

"Let us watch more closely and let us see the Princess Hilnaric in the season of the orchard-bloom when the great birds go by that know the Sea, to rest in our inland places; and if she be more beautiful than the sunrise over our folded kingdoms when all the orchards bloom, it may be that she is more beautiful than the Sea."

And the King of Arizim said:

"I fear this is terrible blasphemy, yet will I do as you have decided in council."

And the season of the orchard-bloom appeared. One night the King of Arizim called his daughter forth on his outer balcony of marble. And the moon was rising huge and round and holy over dark woods, and all the fountains were singing to the night. And the moon touched the marble palace gables, and they glowed in the land. And the moon touched the heads of all the fountains, and the grey columns broke into fairy lights. And the moon left the dark ways of the forest and lit the whole white palace and its fountains and shone on the forehead of the Princess, and the palace of Arizim glowed afar, and the fountains became columns of gleaming jewels and song. And the moon made a music at its rising, but it fell a little short of mortal ears. And Hilnaric stood there wondering, clad in white, with the moonlight shining on her forehead; and watching her from the shadows on the terrace stood the kings of Mondath and Toldees.

They said: "She is more beautiful than the moonrise." And the sea-son of the orchard-bloom appeared. And on another day the King of Arizim bade his daughter forth at dawn, and they stood again upon the balcony. And the sun came up over a world of orchards, and the sea-mists went back over Poltarnees to the Sea; little wild voices arose in all the thickets, the voices of the fountains began to die, and the song arose, in all the marble temples, of the birds that are sacred to the Sea. And Hilnaric stood there, still glowing with dreams of heaven.

"She is more beautiful," said the kings, "than morning."

Yet one more trial they made of Hilnaric's beauty, for they watched her on the terraces at sunset ere yet the petals of the orchards had fallen, and all along the edge of neighbouring woods the rhododendron was blooming with the azalea. And the sun went down under craggy Poltarnees, and the sea-mist poured over his summit inland. And the marble temples stood up clear in the evening, but films of twilight were drawn between the mountain and the city. Then from the Temple ledges and eaves of palaces the bats fell headlong downwards, then spread their wings and floated up and down through darkening ways; lights came blinking out in golden windows, men cloaked themselves against the grey sea-mist, the sound of small songs arose, and the face of Hilnaric became a resting-place for mysteries and dreams.

"Than all these things," said the kings, "she is more lovely: but who can say whether she is lovelier than the Sea?"

Prone in a rhododendron thicket at the edge of the palace lawns a hunter had waited since the sun went down. Near to him was a deep pool where the hyacinths grew and strange flowers floated upon it with broad leaves; and there the great bull gariachs[8] came down to drink by star-light; and, waiting there for the gariachs to come, he saw the white form of the Princess leaning on her balcony. Before the stars shone out or the bulls came down to drink he left his lurking-place and moved closer to the palace to see more nearly the Princess. The palace lawns were full of untrodden dew, and everything was still when he came across them, holding his great spear. In the farthest corner of the terraces the three old kings were discussing the beauty of Hilnaric and the destiny of the Inner Lands. Moving lightly, with a hunter's tread, the watcher by the pool came very near, even in the still evening, before the Princess saw him. When he saw her closely he exclaimed suddenly:

"She must be more beautiful than the Sea."

When the Princess turned and saw his garb and his great spear she knew that he was a hunter of gariachs.

When the three kings heard the young man exclaim they said softly to one another:

"This must be the man."

Then they revealed themselves to him, and spoke to him to try him. They said:

"Sir, you have spoken blasphemy against the Sea."

---

[8] A fictional beast invented by Dunsany. Given the sound of the word Dunsany is probably drawing on the extinct European species of Bison, the Aurochs.

And the young man muttered:

"She is more beautiful than the Sea."

And the kings said:

"We are older than you and wiser, and know that nothing is more beautiful than the Sea."

And the young man took off the gear of his head, and became downcast, and he knew that he spake with kings, yet he answered:

"By this spear, she is more beautiful than the Sea."

And all the while the Princess stared at him, knowing him to be a hunter of gariachs.

Then the king of Arizim said to the watcher by the pool:

"If thou wilt go up Poltarnees and come back, as none have come, and report to us what lure or magic is in the Sea, we will pardon thy blasphemy, and thou shalt have the Princess to wife and sit among the Council of Kings."[9]

And gladly thereunto the young man consented. And the Princess spoke to him, and asked him his name. And he told her that his name was Athelvok, and great joy arose in him at the sound of her voice. And to the three kings he promised to set out on the third day to scale the slope of Poltarnees and to return again, and this was the oath by which they bound him to return:

---

[9] Nobody seems to have asked the princess how she felt about this...

"I swear by the Sea that bears the worlds away, by the river of Oriathon, which men call Ocean, and by the gods and their tiger, and by the doom of the worlds, that I will return again to the Inner Lands, having beheld the Sea."

And that oath he swore with solemnity that very night in one of the temples of the Sea, but the three kings trusted more to the beauty of Hilnaric even than to the power of the oath.

The next day Athelvok came to the palace of Arizim with the morning, over the fields to the East and out of the country of Toldees, and Hilnaric came out along her balcony and met him on the terraces. And she asked him if he had ever slain a gariach, and he said that he had slain three, and then he told her how he had killed his first down by the pool in the wood. For he had taken his father's spear and gone down to the edge of the pool, and had lain under the azaleas there waiting for the stars to shine, by whose first light the gariachs go to the pools to drink; and he had gone too early and had had long to wait, and the passing hours seemed longer than they were. And all the birds came in that home at night, and the bat was abroad, and the hour of the duck went by, and still no gariach came down to the pool; and Athelvok felt sure that none would come. And just as this grew to a certainty in his mind the thicket parted noiselessly and a huge bull gariach stood facing him on the edge of the water, and his great horns swept out sideways from his head, and at the

13

ends curved upwards, and were four strides in width from tip to tip. And he had not seen Athelvok, for the great bull was on the far side of the little pool, and Athelvok could not creep round to him for fear of meeting the wind (for the gariachs, who can see little in the dark forests, rely on hearing and smell). But he devised swiftly in his mind while the bull stood there with head erect just twenty strides from him across the water. And the bull sniffed the wind cautiously and listened, then lowered his great head down to the pool and drank. At that instant Athelvok leapt into the water and shot forward through its weedy depths among the stems of the strange flowers that floated upon broad leaves on the surface. And Athelvok kept his spear out straight before him, and the fingers of his left hand he held rigid and straight, not pointing upwards, and so did not come to the surface, but was carried onward by the strength of his spring and passed unentangled through the stems of the flowers. When Athelvok jumped into the water the bull must have thrown his head up, startled at the splash, then he would have listened and have sniffed the air, and neither hearing nor scenting any danger he must have remained rigid for some moments, for it was in that attitude that Athelvok found him as he emerged breathless at his feet. And, striking at once, Athelvok drove the spear into his throat before the head and the terrible horns came down. But Athelvok had clung to one of the great horns,

14

and had been carried at terrible speed through the rhododendron bushes until the gariach fell, but rose at once
again, and died standing up, still struggling, drowned in its
own blood.

But to Hilnaric listening it was as though one of the
heroes of old time had come back again in the full glory
of his legendary youth.

And long time they went up and down the terraces,
saying those things which were said before and since, and
which lips shall yet be made to say again. And above them
stood Poltarnees beholding the Sea.

And the day came when Athelvok should go. And
Hilnaric said to him:

"Will you not indeed most surely come back again,
having just looked over the summit of Poltarnees?"

Athelvok answered: "I will indeed come back, for thy
voice is more beautiful than the hymn of the priests when
they chant and praise the Sea, and though many tributary
seas ran down into Oriathon and he and all the others
poured their beauty into one pool below me, yet would I
return swearing that thou were fairer than they."

And Hilnaric answered:

"The wisdom of my heart tells me, or old knowledge
or prophecy, or some strange lore, that I shall never hear
thy voice again. And for this I give thee my forgiveness."

But he, repeating the oath that he had sworn, set out,
looking often backwards until the slope became to step

and his face was set to the rock. It was in the morning that he started, and he climbed all the day with little rest, where every foot-hole was smooth with many feet. Before he reached the top the sun disappeared from him, and darker and darker grew the Inner Lands. Then he pushed on so as to see before dark whatever thing Poltarnees had to show. The dusk was deep over the Inner Lands, and the lights of cities twinkled through the sea-mist when he came to Poltarnees' summit, and the sun before him was not yet gone from the sky.

And there below him was the old wrinkled Sea, smiling and murmuring song. And he nursed little ships with gleaming sails, and in his hands were old regretted wrecks, and mast all studded over with golden nails that he had rent in anger out of beautiful galleons. And the glory of the sun was among the surges as they brought driftwood out of isles of spice, tossing their golden heads. And the grey currents crept away to the south like companionless serpents that love something afar with a restless, deadly love. And the whole plain of water glittering with late sunlight, and the surges and the currents and the white sails of ships were all together like the face of a strange new god that has looked at a man for the first time in the eyes at the moment of his death; and Athelvok, looking on the wonderful Sea, knew why it was that the dead never return, for there is something that the dead feel and know, and the living would never understand even though the dead should come and speak to them about it. And there was the Sea smiling at him, glad with the glory of the sun. And there was a haven there for homing ships, and a sunlit city stood upon its marge, and people walked about the streets of it clad in the unimagined merchandise of far sea-bordering lands.

An easy slope of loose rock went from the top of Poltarnees to the shore of the Sea.

For a long while Athelvok stood there regretfully, knowing that there had come something into his soul that no one in the Inner Lands could understand, where the thoughts of their minds had gone no farther than the three little kingdoms. Then, looking long upon the wandering ships, and the marvelous merchandise from alien lands, and the unknown colour that wreathed the brows of the Sea, he turned his face to the darkness and the Inner Lands.

At that moment the Sea sang a dirge at sunset for all the harm that he had done in anger and all the ruin wrought on adventurous ships; and there were tears in the voice of the tyrannous Sea, for he had loved the galleons that he had overwhelmed, and he called all men to him and all living things that he might make amends, because he had loved the bones that he had strewn afar. And Athelvok turned and set one foot upon the crumbled slope, and then another, and walked a little way to be nearer to the Sea, and then a dream came upon him and he felt that men had wronged the lovely Sea because he had been angry a little, because he had been sometimes cruel; he felt that there was trouble among the tides of the Sea because he had loved the galleons who were dead. Still he walked on and the crumbled stones rolled with him, and just as the twilight faded and a star appeared he came to the golden shore, and walked on till the surges were about his knees, and he heard the prayer-like blessings of the Sea. Long he stood thus, while the stars came out above him and shone again in the surges; more stars came wheeling in their courses up from the Sea, lights twinkled out through all the haven city, lanterns were slung from the ships, the purple night burned on; and Earth, to the eyes of the gods as they sat afar, glowed as with one flame. Then Athelvok went into the haven city; there he met many who had left the Inner Lands before him; none of them wished to return to the people who had not seen the Sea; many of them had forgotten the three little kingdoms, and it was rumoured that one man, who had once tried to return, had found the shifting, crumbled slope impossible to climb.

Hilnaric never married. But her dowry was set aside to build a temple wherein men curse the ocean.

Once every year, with solemn rite and ceremony, they curse the tides of the Sea; and the moon looks in and hates them.

Blagdaross

On a waste place strewn with bricks in the outskirts of a town twilight was falling. A star or two appeared over the smoke, and distant windows lit mysterious lights. The stillness deepened and the loneliness. Then all the outcast things that are silent by day found voices.

An old cork[10] spoke first. He said: "I grew in Andalusian woods, but never listened to the idle songs of Spain. I only grew strong in the sunlight waiting for my destiny. One day the merchants came and took us all away and carried us all along the shore of the sea, piled high on the backs of donkeys, and in a town by the sea they made me into the shape that I am now. One day they sent me northward to Provence[11], and there I fulfilled my destiny. For they set me as a guard over the bubbling wine, and I faithfully stood sentinel for twenty years. For the first few years in the bottle that I guarded the wine slept, dreaming of Provence; but as the years went on he grew stronger and stronger, until at last whenever a man went by the wind would put out all his might against me, saying, 'Let me go free; let me go free!' And every year his strength increased,

---

[10] Yes, an actual bottle cork.
[11] A region in southeastern France famous for its wine.

and he grew more clamourous when men went by, but never availed to hurl me from my post. But when I had powerfully held him for twenty years they brought him to the banquet and took me from my post, and the wine arose rejoicing and leapt through the veins of men and exalted their souls within them till they stood up in their places and sang Provençal songs. But me they cast away— me that had been sentinel for twenty years, and was still as strong and staunch as when first I went on guard. Now I am an outcast in a cold northern city, who once have known the Andalusian skies and guarded long ago Provençal suns that swam in the heart of the rejoicing wine."

An unstruck match that somebody had dropped spoke next. "I am a child of the sun," he said, "and an enemy of cities; there is more in my heart than you know of. I am a brother of Etna and Stromboli[12]; I have fires lurking in me that will one day rise up beautiful and strong. We will not go into servitude on any hearth nor work machines for our food, but we will take out own food where we find it on that day when we are strong. There are wonderful children in my heart whose faces shall be more lively than the rainbow; they shall make a compact with the North wind, and he shall lead them forth; all shall be black behind them and black above them, and there shall

---

[12] Active volcanoes located in Italy.

be nothing beautiful in the world but them; they shall seize upon the earth and it shall be theirs, and nothing shall stop them but our old enemy the sea."

Then an old broken kettle spoke, and said: "I am the friend of cities. I sit among the slaves upon the hearth, the little flames that have been fed with coal. When the slaves dance behind the iron bars I sit in the middle of the dance and sing and make our masters glad. And I make songs about the comfort of the cat, and about the malice that is towards her in the heart of the dog, and about the crawling of the baby, and about the ease that is in the lord of the house when we brew the good brown tea; and sometimes when the house is very warm and slaves and masters are glad, I rebuke the hostile winds that prowl about the world."

And then there spoke the piece of an old cord. "I was made in a place of doom, and doomed men made my fibres, working without hope. Therefore there came a grimness into my heart, so that I never let anything go free when once I was set to bind it. Many a thing have I bound relentlessly for months and years; for I used to come coiling into warehouses where the great boxes lay all open to the air, and one of them would be suddenly closed up, and my fearful strength would be set on him like accurse, and if his timbers groaned when first I seized them, or if they creaked aloud in the lonely night, thinking of wood-lands out of which they came, then I only gripped them tighter still, for the poor useless hate is in my soul of those that made me in the place of doom. Yet, for all the things that my prison-clutch has held, the last work that I did was to set something free. I lay idle one night in the gloom on the warehouse floor. Nothing stirred there, and even the spider slept. Towards midnight a great flock of echoes suddenly leapt up from the wooden planks and circled round the roof. A man was coming towards me all alone. And as he came his soul was reproaching him, and I saw that there was a great trouble between the man and his soul, for his soul would not let him be, but went on reproaching him.

"Then the man saw me and said, 'This at least will not fail me.' When I heard him say this about me, I determined that whatever he might require of me it should be done to the uttermost. And as I made this determination in my unfaltering heart, he picked me up and stood on an empty box that I should have bound on the morrow, and tied one end of me to a dark rafter; and the knot was carelessly tied, because his soul was reproaching him all the while continually and giving him no ease. Then he made the other end of me into a noose, but when the man's soul saw this it stopped reproaching the man, and cried out to him hurriedly, and besought him to be at peace with it and to do nothing sudden; but the man went on with his work, and put the noose down over his face and underneath his chin, and the soul screamed horribly.

"Then the man kicked the box away with his foot, and the moment he did this I knew that my strength was not great enough to hold him; but I remembered that he had said I would not fail him, and I put all my grim vigour into my fibres and held by sheer will. Then the soul shouted to me to give way, but I said:

"'No; you vexed the man.'

"Then it screamed for me to leave go of the rafter, and already I was slipping, for I only held on to it by a careless knot, but I gripped with my prison grip and said:

"'You vexed the man.'

"And very swiftly it said other things to me, but I answered not; and at last the soul that vexed the man that had trusted me flew away and left him at peace. I was never able to bind things any more, for every one of my fibres was worn and wrenched, and even my relentless heart was weakened by the struggle. Very soon afterwards I was thrown out here. I have done my work."

So they spoke among themselves, but all the while there loomed above them the form of an old rocking-horse complaining bitterly. He said: "I am Blagdaross. Woe is me that I should lie now an outcast among these worthy but little people. Alas! for the days that are gathered, and alas for the Great One that was a master and a soul to me, whose spirit is now shrunken and can never know me again, and no more ride abroad on knightly quests. I was Bucephalus when he was Alexander, and carried him victorious as far as Ind. I encountered dragons with him when he was St. George, I was the horse of Roland fighting for Christendom, and was often Rosinante.[13] I fought in tournays and went errant upon quests, and met Ulysses and the heroes and the fairies. Or late in the evening, just before the lamps in the nursery were put out, he would suddenly mount me, and we would gallop through Africa. There we would pass by night through tropic forests, and come upon dark rivers sweeping by, all gleaming with the eyes of crocodiles, where the hippopotamus floated down with the stream, and mysterious craft loomed suddenly out of the dark and furtively passed away. And when we had passed through the forest lit by the fireflies we would come to the open plains, and gallop onwards with scarlet flamingoes flying along beside us through the lands of dusky kings, with golden crowns upon their heads and scepters in their hands, who came running out of their palaces to see us pass. Then I would wheel suddenly, and the dust flew up from my four hooves as I turned and we galloped home again, and my master was put to bed. And again he would ride abroad on another day till we came to magical fortresses guarded

---

[13] These are all famous horses and their riders.

by wizardry and overthrew the dragons at the gate, and ever came back with a princess fairer than the sea.

"But my master began to grow larger in his body and smaller in his soul, and then he rode more seldom upon quests. At last he saw gold and never came again, and I was cast out here among these little people."

But while the rocking-horse was speaking two boys stole away, un-noticed by their parents, from a house on the edge of the waste place, and were coming across it looking for adventures. One of them carried a broom, and when he saw the rocking-horse he said nothing, but broke off the handle from the broom and thrust it between his braces and his shirt on the left side. Then he mounted the rocking-horse, and drawing forth the broomstick, which was sharp and spiky at the end, said, "Saladin is in this desert with all his paynims[14], and I am Coeur de Lion.[15]" After a while the other boy said: "Now let me kill Saladin too." But Blagdaross in his wooden heart, that exulted with thoughts of battle, said: "I am Blagdaross yet!"

---

[14] A non-Christian, especially a Muslim.
[15] This refers to the Third Crusade, in which Richard the Lionheart of England ("Coeur de Lion" in French) defeated the Ayyubid leader Saladin.

The Madness of Andelsprutz[16]

I had said, "There will be sunlight on it when I see for the first time the beautiful conquered city whose fame has so often made for me lovely dreams." Suddenly I saw its fortifications lifting out of the fields, and behind them stood its belfries. I went in by a gate and saw its houses and streets, and a great disappointment came upon me. For there is an air about a city, and it has a way with it, whereby a man may recognize one from another at once. There are cities full of happiness and cities full of pleasure, and cities full of gloom. There are cities with their faces to heaven, and some with their faces to earth; some have a way of looking at the past and others look at the future; some notice you if you come among them, others glance at you, others let you go by. Some love the cities that are their neighbours, others are dear to the plains and to the heath; some cities are bare to the wind, others have purple cloaks and others brown cloaks, and some are clad in white. Some tell the old tale of their infancy, with others

---

[16] Andel in most Scandinavian languages means "proportion" or "share" and sprutz is so phonetically close to "spirits" that this could easily be Dunsany amusing himself linguistically by calling the town Share (or proportion) of Spirits.

it is secret; some cities sing and some mutter, some are angry, and some have broken hearts, and each city has her way of greeting Time.

I had said: "I will see Andelsprutz arrogant with her beauty," and I had said: "I will see her weeping over her conquest."

I had said: "She will sing songs to me," and "she will be reticent," "she will be all robed," and "she will be bare but splendid."

But the windows of Andelsprutz in her houses looked vacantly over the plains like the eyes of a dead madman. At the hour her chimes sounded unlovely and discordant, some of them were out of tune, and the bells of some were cracked, her roofs were bald and without moss. At evening no pleasant rumour arose in her streets. When the lamps were lit in the houses no mystical flood of light stole out into the dusk, you merely saw that there were lighted lamps; Andelsprutz had no way with her and no air about her. When the night fell and the blinds were all drawn down, then I perceived what I had not thought in the daylight. I knew then that Andelsprutz was dead.

I saw a fair-haired man who drank beer in a café, and I said to him:

"Why is the city of Andelsprutz quite dead, and her soul gone hence?"

He answered: "Cities do not have souls[17] and there is never any life in bricks."

And I said to him: "Sir, you have spoken truly."

And I asked the same question of another man, and he gave me the same answer, and I thanked him for his courtesy. And I saw a man of a more slender build, who had black hair, and channels in his cheeks for tears to run in, and I said to him:

"Why is Andelsprutz quite dead, and when did her soul go hence?"

And he answered: "Andelsprutz hoped too much. For thirty years would she stretch out her arms toward the land of Akla every night, to Mother Akla from whom she had been stolen. Every night she would be hoping and sighing, and stretching out her arms to Mother Akla. At midnight, once a year, on the anniversary of the terrible day, Akla would send spies to lay a wreath against the walls of Andelsprutz. She could do no more. And on this night, once in every year, I used to weep, for weeping was the mood of the city that nursed me. Every night while other cities slept did Andelsprutz sit brooding here and hoping, till

---

[17] As we saw in Blagdaross a major theme of Dreamer's Tales is to consider the souls of things we often thing of as soulless, to look at our world not as full of inanimate objects but rather wholly animate. While Dunsany does this literally, it's part of the overarching ethos the pervades his work to move a little more slowly, take the world in a little bit more deeply and experience it more richly.

thirty wreaths lay mouldering by her walls, and still the armies of Akla could not come.

"But after she had hoped so long, and on the night that faithful spies had brought her thirtieth wreath, Andelsprutz went suddenly mad. All the bells clanged hideously in the belfries, horses bolted in the streets, the dogs all howled, the stolid conquerors awoke and turned in their beds and slept again; and I saw the grey shadowy form of Andelsprutz rise up, decking her hair with the phantasms of cathedrals, and stride away from her city. And the great shadowy form that was the soul of Andelsprutz went away muttering to the mountains, and there I followed her—for had she not been my nurse? Yes, I went away alone into the mountains, and for three days, wrapped in a cloak, I slept in their misty solitudes. I had no food to eat, and to drink I had only the water of the mountain streams. By day no living thing was near to me, and I heard nothing but the noise of the wind, and the mountain streams roaring. But for three nights I heard all round me on the mountain the sounds of a great city: I saw the lights of tall cathedral windows flash momentarily on the peaks, and at times the glimmering lantern of some fortress patrol. And I saw the huge misty outline of the soul of Andelsprutz sitting decked with her ghostly cathedrals, speaking to herself, with her eyes fixed before her in a mad stare, telling of ancient wars. And her confused speech for all those nights upon the mountain was sometimes the voice of traffic, and then of church bells, and then of bugles, but oftenest it was the voice of red war; and it was all incoherent, and she was quite mad.

"The third night it rained heavily all night long, but I stayed up there to watch the soul of my native city. And she still sat staring straight before her, raving; but here voice was gentler now, there were more chimes in it, and occasional song. Midnight passed, and the rain still swept down on me, and still the solitudes of the mountain were full of the mutterings of the poor mad city. And the hours after mid-night came, the cold hours wherein sick men die.

"Suddenly I was aware of great shapes moving in the rain, and heard the sound of voices that were not of my city nor yet of any that I ever knew. And presently I discerned, though faintly, the souls of a great concourse of cities, all bending over Andelsprutz and comforting her, and the ravines of the mountains roared that night with the voices of cities that had lain still for centuries. For there came the soul of Camelot that had so long ago forsaken Usk[18]; and there was Ilion[19], all girt with towers, still

---

[18] Usk is a Welsh town. Interestingly Dunsany is saying that it used to be Camelot, until the soul of Camelot fled, leaving it to remain as the rather ordinary town of Usk.
[19] Ilion is the old name for Troy (and the reason the Iliad is called the Iliad).

cursing the sweet face of ruinous Helen; I saw there Babylon and Persepolis[20], and the bearded face of bull-like Nineveh[21], and Athens mourning her immortal gods.

"All these souls if cities that were dead spoke that night on the mountain to my city and soothed her, until at last she muttered of war no longer, and her eyes stared wildly no more, but she hid her face in her hands and for some while wept softly. At last she arose, and walking slowly and with bended head, and leaning upon Ilion and Carthage[22], went mournfully eastwards; and the dust of her highways swirled behind her as she went, a ghostly dust that never turned to mud in all that drenching rain. And so the souls of the cities led her away, and gradually they disappeared from the mountain, and the ancient voices died away in the distance.

"Not since then have I seen my city alive; but once I met with a traveler who said that somewhere in the midst of a great desert are gathered together the souls of all dead cities. He said that he was lost once in a place where there was no water, and he heard their voices speaking all the night."

But I said: "I was once without water in a desert and heard a city speaking to me, but knew not whether it really

---

[20] The ruined capitol of the Achaemenid Empire.
[21] An Assyrian city made bearded and bull-like by its Lamassu.
[22] Famously destroyed by the Romans in the Punic Wars.

spoke to me or not, for on that day I heard so many terrible things, and only some of them were true."

And the man with the black hair said: "I believe it to be true, though whither she went I know not. I only know that a shepherd found me in the morning faint with hunger and cold, and carried me down here; and when I came to Andelsprutz it was, as you have perceived it, dead."

Where the Tides Ebb and Flow[23]

I dreamt that I had done a horrible thing, so that burial was to be denied me either in soil or sea, neither could there be any hell for me[24].

I waited for some hours, knowing this. Then my friends came for me, and slew me secretly and with ancient rite, and lit great tapers, and carried me away.

It was all in London[25] that the thing was done, and they went furtively at dead of night along grey streets and among mean houses until they came to the river. And the river and the tide of the sea were grappling with one another between the mud-banks, and both of them were black and full of lights. A sudden wonder came in to the eyes of each, as my friends came near to them with their glaring tapers. All these things I saw as they carried me dead and stiffening, for my soul was still among my bones,

---

[23] Dreamer's Tales was the first work of Dunsany's that H.P. Lovecraft read and it had a profound effect on him. In this story I think we can very clearly see why.

[24] Dunsany is intentionally trying to use the reader's own morbid curiosity to hook them. He wants you to *want* to find out what act could be so heinous that not even hell would take the perpetrator.

[25] Many of Dunsany's grimmer stories are set in the real world and attempt to make the real world seem fantastic, rather than the fantastic seem real.

because there was no hell for it, and because Christian burial was denied me.

They took me down a stairway that was green with slimy things, and so came slowly to the terrible mud. There, in the territory of forsaken things, they dug a shallow grave. When they had finished they laid me in the grave, and suddenly they cast their tapers to the river. And when the water had quenched the flaring lights the tapers looked pale and small as they bobbed upon the tide, and at once the glamour of the calamity was gone, and I noticed then the approach of the huge dawn; and my friends cast their cloaks over their faces, and the solemn procession was turned into many fugitives that furtively stole away.

Then the mud came back wearily and covered all but my face. There I lay alone with quite forgotten things, with drifting things that the tides will take no farther, with useless things and lost things, and with the horrible unnatural bricks that are neither stone nor soil. I was rid of feeling, because I had been killed, but perception and thought were in my unhappy soul. The dawn widened, and I saw the desolate houses that crowded the marge of the river, and their dead windows peered into my dead eyes, windows with bales behind them instead of human souls. I grew so weary looking at these forlorn things that I wanted to cry out, but could not, because I was dead. Then I knew, as I had never known before, that for all the years that herd of desolate houses had wanted to cry out too, but, being dead, were dumb. And I knew then that it had yet been well with the forgotten drifting things if they had wept, but they were eyeless and without life. And I, too, tried to weep, but there were no tears in my dead eyes. And I knew then that the river might have cared for us, might have caressed us, might have sung to us, but he swept broadly onwards, thinking of nothing but the princely ships.

At last the tide did what the river would not, and came and covered me over, and my soul had rest in the green water, and rejoiced and believed that it had the Burial of the Sea. But with the ebb the water fell again, and left me alone again with the callous mud among the forgotten things that drift no more, and with the sight of all those desolate houses, and with the knowledge among all of us that each was dead.

In the mournful wall behind me, hung with green weeds, forsaken of the sea, dark tunnels appeared, and secret narrow passages that were clamped and barred. From these at last the stealthy rats came down to nibble me away, and my soul rejoiced thereat and believed that he would be free perforce from the accursed bones to which burial was refused. Very soon the rats ran away a little space and whispered among themselves. They never came any more. When I found that I was accursed even among the rats I tried to weep again.

Then the tide came swinging back and covered the dreadful mud, and hid the desolate houses, and soothed the forgotten things, and my soul had ease for a while in the sepulture of the sea. And then the tide forsook me again.

To and fro it came about me for many years. Then the County Council found me, and gave me decent burial. It was the first grave that I had ever slept in. That very night my friends[26] came for me. They dug me up and put me back again in the shallow hold in the mud.

Again and again through the years my bones found burial, but al-ways behind the funeral lurked one of those terrible men who, as soon as night fell, came and dug them up and carried them back again to the hole in the mud.

And then one day the last of those men died who once had done to me this terrible thing. I heard his soul go over the river at sunset.

And again I hoped.

A few weeks afterwards I was found once more, and once more taken out of that restless place and given deep burial in sacred ground, where my soul hoped that it should rest.

---

[26] The continued insistence on these being his "friends" makes the tale that much more horrible

Almost at once men came with cloaks and tapers to give me back to the mud, for the thing had become a tradition and a rite. And all the forsaken things mocked me in their dumb hearts when they saw me carried back, for they were jealous of me because I had left the mud. It must be remembered that I could not weep.

And the years went by seawards where the black barges go, and the great derelict centuries became lost at sea, and still I lay there without any cause to hope, and daring not to hope without a cause, because of the terrible envy and the anger of the things that could drift no more.

Once a great storm rode up, even as far as London, out of the sea from the South; and he came curving into the river with the fierce East wind. And he was mightier than the dreary tides, and went with great leaps over the listless mud. And all the sad forgotten things rejoiced, and mingled with things that were haughtier than they, and rode once more amongst the lordly shipping that was driven up and down. And out of their hideous home he took my bones, never again, I hoped, to be vexed with the ebb and flow. And with the fall of the tide he went riding down the river and turned to the southwards, and so went to his home. And my bones he scattered among many isles and along the shores of happy alien mainlands. And for a moment, while they were far asunder, my soul was almost free.

Then there arose, at the will of the moon, the assiduous flow of the tide, and it undid at once the work of the ebb, and gathered my bones from the marge of sunny isles, and gleaned them all along the main-land's shores, and went rocking northwards till it came to the mouth of the Thames, and there turned westwards its relentless face, and so went up the river and came to the hole in the mud, and into it dropped my bones; and partly the mud covered them, and partly it left them white, for the mud cares not for its forsaken things.

Then the ebb came, and I saw the dead eyes of the houses and the jealousy of the other forgotten things that the storm had not carried thence.

And some more centuries passed over the ebb and flow and over the loneliness of things for gotten. And I lay there all the while in the careless grip of the mud, never wholly covered, yet never able to go free, and I longed for the great caress of the warm Earth or the comfortable lap of the Sea.

Sometimes men found my bones and buried them, but the tradition never died, and my friends' successors always brought them back. At last the barges went no more, and there were fewer lights; shaped timbers no longer floated down the fairway, and there came instead old wind-up-rooted trees in all their natural simplicity.

At last I was aware that somewhere near me a blade of grass was growing, and the moss began to appear all over the dead houses. One day some thistledown went drifting over the river.

For some years I watched these signs attentively, until I became certain that London was passing away. Then I hoped once more, and all along both banks of the river there was anger among the lost things that anything should dare to hope upon the forsaken mud. Gradually the horrible houses crumbled, until the poor dead things that never had had life got decent burial among the weeds and moss. At last the may appeared and the convolvulus[27]. Finally, the wild rose stood up over mounds that had been wharves and warehouses. Then I knew that the cause of Nature had triumphed, and London had passed away.

The last man in London came to the wall by the river, in an ancient cloak that was one of those that once my friends had worn, and peered over the edge to see that I still was there. Then he went, and I never saw men again: they had passed away with London.

A few days after the last man had gone the birds came into London, all the birds that sing. When they first saw me they all looked sideways at me, then they went away a little and spoke among themselves.

---

[27] May here refers to mayflowers, and convolvulus are morning glories.

"He only sinned against Man," they said; "it is not our quarrel."

"Let us be kind to him," they said.

Then they hopped nearer me and began to sing. It was the time of the rising of the dawn, and from both banks of the river, and from the sky, and from the thickets that were once the streets, hundreds of birds were singing. As the light increased the birds sang more and more; they grew thicker and thicker in the air above my head, till there were thousands of them singing there, and then millions, and at last I could see nothing but a host of flickering wings with the sunlight on them, and little gaps of sky. Then when there was nothing to be heard in London but the myriad notes of that exultant song, my soul rose up from the bones in the hole in the mud and began to climb heaven-wards. And it seemed that a lane-way opened amongst the wings of the birds, and it went up and up, and one of the smaller gates of Paradise stood ajar at the end of it. And then I knew by a sign that the mud should receive me no more, for suddenly I found that I could weep.

At this moment I opened my eyes in bed in a house in London, and outside some sparrows were twittering in a tree in the light of the radiant morning; and there were tears still wet upon my face, for one's restraint is feeble while one sleeps. But I arose and opened the window wide, and stretching my hands out over the little garden, I blessed the birds whose song had woken me up from the troubled and terrible centuries of my dream.

Bethmoora[28]

There is a faint freshness in the London night as though some strayed reveler of a breeze had left his comrades in the Kentish uplands and had entered the town by stealth. The pavements are a little damp and shiny. Upon one's ears that at this late hour have become very acute there hits the tap of a remote footfall. Louder and louder grow the taps, filling the whole night. And a black cloaked figure passes by, and goes tapping into the dark. One who has danced goes homewards. Somewhere a ball has closed its doors and ended. Its yellow lights are out, its musicians are silent, its dancers have all gone into the night air, and Time has said of it, "Let it be past and over, and among the things that I have put away."

Shadows begin to detach themselves from their great gathering places. No less silently than those shadows that are thin and dead move homewards the stealthy cats. Thus have we even in London our faint forebodings of the

---

[28] Guillermo del Toro has expressed the influence that Dunsany had on him, making it somewhat less surprising that Bethmoora made an appearance in Hellboy 2...

dawn's approach, which the birds and the beasts and the stars are crying aloud to the untrammeled fields.

At what moment I know not I perceive that the night itself is irrevocably overthrown. It is suddenly revealed to me by the weary pallor of the street lamps that the streets are silent and nocturnal still, not because there is any strength in night, but because men have not yet arisen from sleep to defy him. So have I seen dejected and untidy guards still bearing antique muskets in palatial gateways, although the realms of the monarch that they guard have shrunk to a single province which no enemy yet has troubled to overrun.

And it is now manifest from the aspect of the street lamps, those abashed dependants of night, that already English mountain peaks have seen the dawn, that the cliffs of Dover are standing white to the morning, that the sea-mist has lifted and is pouring inland.

And now men with a hose have come and are sluicing out the streets.

Behold now night is dead.

What memories, what fancies throng one's mind! A night but just now gathered out of London by the horrific hand of Time. A million common artificial things all cloaked for a while in mystery, like beggars robed in purple[29], and seated on dread thrones. Four million people asleep, dreaming perhaps. What worlds have they gone into? Whom have they met? But my thoughts are far off with Bethmoora[30] in her loneliness, whose gates swing to and fro. To and fro they swing, and creak and creak in the wind, but no one hears them. They are of green copper, very lovely, but no one sees them now. The desert wind pours sand into their hinges, no watchman comes to ease them. No guard goes round Bethmoora's battlements, no enemy assails them. There are no lights in her houses, no footfall on her streets, she stands there dead and lonely beyond the Hills of Hap, and I would see Bethmoora once again, but dare not.

It is many a year, they tell me, since Bethmoora became desolate.

Her desolation is spoken of in taverns where sailors meet, and certain travellers have told me of it.

I had hoped to see Bethmoora once again. It is many a year ago, they say, when the vintage was last gathered in from the vineyards that I knew, where it is all desert now. It was a radiant day, and the people of the city were dancing by the vineyards, while here and there one played upon

---

[29] The imperial color of Rome.
[30] In *The Whisperer in Darkness* Lovecraft purloins Bethmoora and includes it in the list of things that exist within his mythos.

the kalipac[31]. The purple flowering shrubs were all in bloom, and the snow shone upon the Hills of Hap.

Outside the copper gates they crushed the grapes in vats to make the syrabub[32]. It had been a goodly vintage.

In the little gardens at the desert's edge men beat the tambang and the tittibuk, and blew melodiously the zooti-bar[33].

All there was mirth and song and dance, because the vintage had been gathered in, and there would be ample syrabub for the winter months, and much left over to ex-change for turquoises and emeralds with the merchants who come down from Oxuhahn. Thus they rejoiced all day over their vintage on the narrow strip of cultivated ground that lay between Bethmoora and the desert which meets the sky to the South. And when the heat of the day began to abate, and the sun drew near to the snows on the Hills of Hap, the note of the zootibar still rose clear from the gardens, and the brilliant dresses of the dancers still wound among the flowers. All that day three men on

---

[31] Not an instrument in our world

[32] While Syrabub not a real drink, Dunsany might have been trying to evoke in his readers Syllabub: a popular 19th century drink made of cream curdled by wine and then sweetened.

[33] None of these are instruments in our world either. Though amus-ingly, because Dunsany was associated with the Irish Renaissance people started to mistakenly claim these were traditional Irish instru-ments.

mules had been noticed crossing the face of the Hills of Hap. Backwards and forwards they moved as the track wound lower and lower, three little specks of black against the snow. They were seen first in the very early morning up near the shoulder of Peol Jagganoth, and seemed to be coming out of Utnar Véhi. All day they came. And in the evening, just before the lights come out and colours change, they appeared before Bethmoora's copper gates. They carried staves, such as messengers bear in those lands, and seemed sombrely clad when the dancers all came round them with their green and lilac dresses. Those Europeans who were present and heard the message given were ignorant of the language, and only caught the name of Utnar Véhi. But it was brief, and passed rapidly from mouth to mouth, and almost at once the people burnt their vineyards and began to flee away from Bethmoora, going for the most part northwards, though some went to the East. They ran down out of their fair white houses, and streamed through the copper gate; the throbbing of the tambang and the tittibuk suddenly ceased with the note of the Zootibar, and the clinking kalipac stopped a moment after. The three strange travellers went back the way they came the instant their message was given. It was the hour when a light would have appeared in some high tower, and window after window would have poured into the dusk its lion-frightening light, and the cooper gates would have been fastened up. But no lights came out in

46

windows there that night and have not ever since, and those copper gates were left wide and have never shut, and the sound arose of the red fire crackling in the vineyards, and the pattering of feet fleeing softly. There were no cries, no other sounds at all, only the rapid and determined flight. They fled as swiftly and quietly as a herd of wild cattle flee when they suddenly see a man. It was as though something had befallen which had been feared for generations, which could only be escaped by instant flight, which left no time for indecision.

Then fear took the Europeans also, and they too fled. And what the message was I have never heard.

Many believe that it was a message from Thuba Mleen[34], the myste-rious emperor of those lands, who is never seen by man, advising that Bethmoora should be left desolate. Others say that the message was one of warning from the gods, whether from friendly gods or from adverse ones they know not.

And others hold that the Plague was ravaging a line of cities over in Utnar Véhi, following the South-west wind which for many weeks had been blowing across them towards Bethmoora.

---

[34] Interestingly, Thuba Mleen made his way into 2nd edition Dungeons and Dragons via the TSR trading cards…where he was mistakenly conflated with the King in Yellow. But in case you were wondering: he's a 20th level Psionicist.

Some say that the terrible gnousar[35] sickness was upon the three travellers, and that their very mules were dripping with it, and suppose that they were driven to the city by hunger, but suggest no better reason for so terrible a crime.

But most believe that it was a message from the desert himself[36], who owns all the Earth to the southwards, spoken with his peculiar cry to those three who knew his voice—men who had been out on the sand-wastes without tents by night, who had been by day without water, men who had been out there where the desert mutters, and had grown to know his needs and his malevolence. They say that the desert had a need for Bethmoora, that he wished to come into her lovely streets, and to send into her temples and her houses his storm-winds draped with sand. For he hates the sound and the sight of men in his old evil heart, and he would have Bethmoora silent and undisturbed, save for the weird love he whispers to her gates.

If I knew what that message was that the three men brought on mules, and told in the copper gate, I think that I should go and see Bethmoora once again. For a great longing comes on me here in London to see once more

---

[35] An invention of Dunsany's.

[36] This is another instance of Dunsany personifying the inanimate.

that white and beautiful city, and yet I dare not, for I know not the danger I should have to face, whether I should risk the fury of unknown dreadful gods, or some disease unspeakable and slow, or the desert's curse or torture in some little private room of the Emperor Thuba Mleen, or something that the travelers have not told—perhaps more fearful still.

Idle Days on the Yann[37]

So I came down through the wood on the bank of Yann and found, as had been prophesied, the ship Bird of the River about to loose her cable.

The captain sat cross-legged upon the white deck with his scimitar lying beside him in its jeweled scabbard, and the sailors toiled to spread the nimble sails to bring the ship into the central stream of Yann, and all the while sang ancient soothing songs. And the wind of the evening descending cool from the snowfields of some mountainous abode of distant gods came suddenly, like glad tidings to an anxious city, into the wing-like sails.

And so we came into the central stream, whereat the sailors lowered the greater sails. But I had gone to bow before the captain, and to inquire concerning the miracles, and appearances among men, of the most holy gods of whatever land he had come from[38]. And the captain answered that he came from fair Belzoond, and worshipped gods that were the least and humblest, who seldom sent

---

[37] H.P. Lovecraft's *The White Ship* is loosely based on this story.
[38] Religion and the exploration of religious ideas will play a central part in this story. It's worth taking note of the different ways gods appear or worship is practiced as you read through.

the famine or the thunder, and were easily appeased with little battles. And I told how I came from Ireland, which is of Europe, whereat the captain and all the sailors laughed, for they said, "There are no such places in all the land of dreams." When they had ceased to mock me, I explained that my fancy mostly dwelt in the desert of Cuppar-Nombo, about a beautiful blue city called Golthoth[39] the Damned, which was sentinelled all round by wolves and their shadows, and had been utterly desolate for years and years, because of a curse which the gods once spoke in anger and could never since recall. And sometimes my dreams took me as far as Pungar Vees, the red walled city where the fountains are, which trades with the Isles and Thul[40]. When I said this they complimented me upon the abode of my fancy, saying that, though they had never seen these cities, such places might well be imagined. For the rest of that evening I bargained with the captain over the sum that I should pay him for any fare if God and the tide of Yann should bring us safely as far as the cliffs by the sea, which are named Bar-Wul-Yann, the Gate of Yann.

---

[39] It's hard not to see him as deriving this name from Golgotha, the location of the crucifixion, whose name is often translated as "Place of the Skull"

[40] Probably derivative of Thule, the northmost part of the world according the ancient Greeks, often conflated with Iceland.

And now the sun had set, and all the colours of the world and heaven had held a festival with him, and slipped one by one away before the imminent approach of night. The parrots had all flown home to the jungle on either bank, the monkeys in rows in safety on high branches of the trees were silent and asleep, the fireflies in the deeps of the forest were going up and down, and the great stars came gleaming out to look on the face of Yann. Then the sailors lighted lanterns and hung them round the ship, and the light flashed out on a sudden and dazzled Yann, and the ducks that fed along his marshy banks all suddenly arose, and made wide circles in the upper air, and saw the distant reaches of the Yann and the white mist that softly cloaked the jungle, before they returned again to their marshes.

And then the sailors knelt on the decks and prayed, not all together, but five or six at a time. Side by side there kneeled down together five or six, for there only prayed at the same time men of different faiths, so that no god should hear two men praying to him at once[41]. As soon as any one had finished his prayer, another of the same faith would take his place. Thus knelt the row of five or six with bended heads under the fluttering sail, while the central

---

[41] Dunsany spends much of this story trying to think through the practicalities of a truly pantheistic world, providing minor details like this that are often overlooked in pantheistic fantasy.

stream of the River Yann took them on towards the sea, and their prayers rose up from among the lanterns and went towards the stars. And behind them in the after end of the ship the helmsman prayed aloud the helmsman's prayer, which is prayed by all who follow his trade upon the River Yann, of whatever faith they be. And the captain prayed to his little lesser gods, to the gods that bless Belzoond.

And I too felt that I would pray. Yet I liked not to pray to a jealous God there where the frail affectionate gods whom the heathen love were being humbly invoked; so I bethought me, instead, of Sheol Nugganoth[42], whom the men of the jungle have long since deserted, who is now unworshipped and alone; and to him I prayed.

And upon us praying the night came suddenly down, as it comes upon all men who pray at evening and upon all men who do not; yet our prayers comforted our own souls when we thought of the Great Night to come.

And so Yann bore us magnificently onwards, for he was elate with molten snow that the Poltiades had brought him from the Hills of Hap[43], and the Marn and Migris

---

[42] Here, right after denying the "jealous god" which we can assume to be the Abrahamic god, he chooses instead to worship something with the word Sheol, the old testament land of the dead that was later abandoned for more delineated ideas of heaven and hell, in it.
[43] Establishing that this story exists in the same world as Bethmoora.

were swollen with floods; and he bore us in his full might past Kyph and Pir, and we saw the lights of Goolunza.

Soon we all slept except the helmsman, who kept the ship in the mid-stream of Yann.

When the sun rose the helmsman ceased to sing, for by song he cheered himself in the lonely night. When the song ceased we suddenly all awoke, and another took the helm, and the helmsman slept.

We knew that soon we should come to Mandaroon. We made a meal, and Mandaroon appeared. Then the captain commanded, and the sailors loosed again the greater sails, and the ship turned and left the stream of Yann and came into a harbour beneath the ruddy walls of Mandaroon. Then while the sailors went and gathered fruits I came alone to the gate of Mandaroon. A few huts were outside it, in which lived the guard. A sentinel with a long white beard was standing in the gate, armed with a rusty pike. He wore large spectacles, which were covered with dust. Through the gate I saw the city. A deathly stillness was over all of it. The ways seemed untrodden, and moss was thick on doorsteps; in the market-place huddled figures lay asleep. A scent of incense came wafted through the gateway, of incense and burned poppies, and there was a hum of the echoes of distant bells. I said to the sentinel in the tongue of the region of Yann, "Why are they all asleep in this still city?"

He answered: "None may ask questions in this gate for fear they will wake the people of the city. For when the people of this city wake the gods will die. And when the gods die men may dream no more." And I began to ask him what gods that city worshipped, but he lifted his pike because none might ask questions there. So I left him and went back to the Bird of the River.

Certainly Mandaroon was beautiful with her white pinnacles peering over her ruddy walls and the green of her copper roofs.

When I came back again to the Bird of the River, I found the sailors were returned to the ship. Soon we weighed anchor, and sailed out again, and so came once more to the middle of the river. And now the sun was moving toward his heights, and there had reached us on the River Yann the song of those countless myriads of choirs that attend him in his progress round the world. For the little creatures that have many legs had spread their gauze wings easily on the air, as a man rests his elbows on a balcony and gave jubilant, ceremonial praises to the sun, or else they moved together on the air in wavering dances intricate and swift, or turned aside to avoid the onrush of some drop of water that a breeze had shaken from a jungle orchid, chilling the air and driving it before it, as it fell whirring in its rush to the earth; but all the while they sang triumphantly. "For the day is for us," they said, "whether our great and sacred father the Sun shall bring up more life like us from the marshes, or whether all the world shall end tonight.[44]" And there sang all those whose notes are known to human ears, as well as those whose far more numerous notes have been never heard by man.

To these a rainy day had been as an era of war that should desolate continents during all the lifetime of a man.

And there came out also from the dark and steaming jungle to be-hold and rejoice in the Sun the huge and lazy butterflies. And they danced, but danced idly, on the ways of the air, as some haughty queen of distant conquered lands might in her poverty and exile dance, in some en-campment of the gipsies, for the mere bread to live by, but beyond that would never abate her pride to dance for a fragment more.

And the butterflies sung of strange and painted things, of purple orchids and of lost pink cities and the monstrous colours of the jungle's decay. And they, too, were among those whose voices are not discernible by human ears. And as they floated above the river, going from forest to forest, their splendour was matched by the inimical beauty of the birds who darted out to pursue them. Or sometimes

---

[44] A second theme at play in this work is how we deal with endings. Many of the religions found here have some apocalyptic notion, but Dunsany appears less interested in the apocalypses themselves than how we approach them.

they settled on the white and wax-like blooms of the plant that creeps and clambers about the trees of the forest; and their purple wings flashed out on the great blossoms as, when the caravans go from Nurl to Thace, the gleaming silks flash out upon the snow, where the crafty merchants spread them one by one to astonish the mountaineers of the Hills of Noor.

But upon men and beasts the sun sent drowsiness. The river monsters along the river's marge lay dormant in the slime. The sailors pitched a pavilion, with golden tassels, for the captain upon the deck, and then went, all but the helmsman, under a sail that they had hung as an awning between two masts. Then they told tales to one another, each of his own city or of the miracles of his god, until all were fallen asleep. The captain offered me the shade of his pavillion with the gold tassels, and there we talked for a while, he telling me that he was taking merchandise to Perdóndaris, and that he would take back to fair Belzoond things appertaining to the affairs of the sea. Then, as I watched through the pavilion's opening the brilliant birds and butter-flies that crossed and recrossed over the river, I fell asleep, and dreamed that I was a monarch entering his capital underneath arches of flags, and all the musicians of the world were there, playing melodiously their instruments; but no one cheered.

In the afternoon, as the day grew cooler again, I awoke and found the captain buckling on his scimitar, which he had taken off him while he rested.

And now we were approaching the wide court of Astahahn, which opens upon the river. Strange boats of antique design were chained there to the steps. As we neared it we saw the open marble court, on three sides of which stood the city fronting on colonnades. And in the court and along the colonnades the people of that city walked with solemnity and care according to the rites of ancient ceremony. All in that city was of ancient device; the carving on the houses, which, when age had broken it, remained unrepaired, was of the remotest times, and everywhere were represented in stone beasts that have long since passed away from Earth—the dragon, the griffin, the hippogriffin, and the different species of gargoyle. Nothing was to be found, whether material or custom, that was new in Astahahn. Now they took no notice at all of us as we went by, but continued their processions and ceremonies in the ancient city, and the sailors, knowing their custom, took no notice of them. But I called, as we came near, to one who stood beside the water's edge, asking him what men did in Astahahn and what their merchandise was, and with whom they traded. He said, "Here we have fettered and manacled Time, who would otherwise slay the gods."[45]

I asked him what gods they worshipped in that city, and he said, "All those gods whom Time has not yet slain." Then he turned from me and would say no more, but busied himself in behaving in accordance with ancient custom. And so, according to the will of Yann[46], we drifted onwards and left Astahahn. The river widened below Astahahn, and we found in greater quantities such birds as prey on fishes. And they were very wonderful in their plumage, and they came not out of the jungle, but flew, with their long necks stretched out before them, and their legs lying on the wind behind, straight up the river over the mid-stream.

And now the evening began to gather in. A thick white mist had appeared over the river, and was softly rising higher. It clutched at the trees with long impalpable arms, it rose higher and higher, chilling the air; and white shapes moved away into the jungle as though the ghosts of shipwrecked mariners were searching stealthily in the darkness

---

[45] Another example of an attempt to circumvent an ending.

[46] This can be seen as a juxtaposition. We have the static cities, each in their own way trying to freeze time, next to the ever-moving river (which can be seen as the stream of time) down which he is traveling.

for the spirits of evil that long ago had wrecked them on the Yann.

As the sun sank behind the field of orchids that grew on the matted summit of the jungle, the river monsters came wallowing out of the slime in which they had reclined during the heat of the day, and the great beasts of the jungle came down to drink. The butterflies a while since were gone to rest. In little narrow tributaries that we passed night seemed already to have fallen, though the sun which had disappeared from us had not yet set.

And now the birds of the jungle came flying home far over us, with the sunlight glistening pink upon their breasts, and lowered their pinions as soon as they saw the Yann, and dropped into the trees. And the widgeon began to go up the river in great companies, all whistling, and then would suddenly wheel and all go down again. And there shot by us the small and arrow-like teal; and we heard the manifold cries of flocks of geese, which the sailors told me had recently come in from crossing over the Lispasian ranges; every year they come by the same way, close by the peak of Mluna, leaving it to the left, and the mountain eagles know the way they come and—men say—the very hour, and every year they expect them by the same way as soon as the snows have fallen upon the Northern Plains. But soon it grew so dark that we heard those birds no more, and only heard the whirring of their wings, and of countless others besides, until they all settled

down along the banks of the river, and it was the hour
when the birds of the night went forth. Then the sailors
lit the lanterns for the night, and huge moths appeared,
flapping about the ship, and at moments their gorgeous
colours would be revealed by the lanterns, then they
would pass into the night again, where all was black. And
again the sailors prayed, and thereafter we supped and
slept, and the helmsman took our lives into his care.

When I awoke I found that we had indeed come to
Perdóndaris[47], that famous city. For there it stood upon
the left of us, a city fair and notable, and all the more pleasant for our eyes to see after the jungle that was so long
with us. And we were anchored by the market-place, and
the captain's merchandise was all displayed, and a merchant of Perdóndaris stood looking at it. And the captain
had his scimitar in his hand, and was beating with it in
anger upon the deck, and the splinters were flying up from
the white planks; for the merchant had offered him a price
for his merchandise that the captain declared to be an in-
sult to himself and his country's gods, whom he now said
to be great and terrible gods, whose curses were to be
dreaded. But the merchant waved his hands, which were

---

[47] Perdón is Spanish for "pardon" or "sorry". It's very possible that
this place name is some wordplay on Dunsany's part, further making
light of the ridiculous series of faux-apologies that is about to occur
between the captain and the merchant as they haggle.

of great fatness, showing the pink palms, and swore that of himself he thought not at all, but only of the poor folk in the huts beyond the city to whom he wished to sell the merchandise for as low a price as possible, leaving no remuneration for himself. For the merchandise was mostly the thick toomarund carpets that in the winter keep the wind from the floor, and tollub which the people smoke in pipes. Therefore the merchant said if he offered a piffek more the poor folk must go without their toomarunds when the winter came, and without their tollub in the evenings, or else he and his aged father must starve together. Thereat the captain lifted his scimitar to his own throat, saying that he was now a ruined man, and that nothing remained to him but death. And while he was carefully lifting his beard with his left hand, the merchant eyed the merchandise again, and said that rather than see so worthy a captain die, a man for whom he had conceived an especial love when first he saw the manner in which he handled his ship, he and his aged father should starve together and therefore he offered fifteen piffeks more.

When he said this the captain prostrated himself and prayed to his gods that they might yet sweeten this merchant's bitter heart—to his little lesser gods, to the gods that bless Belzoond.

At last the merchant offered yet five piffeks more. Then the captain wept, for he said that he was deserted of his gods; and the merchant also wept, for he said that he was thinking of his aged father, and of how he soon would starve, and he hid his weeping face with both his hands, and eyed the tollub again between his fingers. And so the bargain was concluded, and the merchant took the too-marund and tollub, paying for them out of a great clinking purse. And these were packed up into bales again, and three of the merchant's slaves carried them upon their heads into the city[48]. And all the while the sailors had sat silent, cross-legged in a crescent upon the deck, eagerly watching the bargain, and now a murmur of satisfaction arose among them, and they began to compare it among themselves with other bargains that they had known. And I found out from them that there are seven merchants in Perdóndaris, and that they had all come to the captain one by one before the bargaining began, and each had warned him privately against the others. And to all the merchants the captain had offered the wine of his own country, that they make in fair Belzoond, but could in no wise persuade them to it. But now that the bargain was over, and the sailors were seated at the first meal of the day, the captain appeared among them with a cask of that wine, and we broached it with care and all made merry together. And

---

[48] If we hadn't already seen through the merchant the "great clinking purse" and "three of the merchant's slaves" are meant to make sure we know exactly what was going on here and put the final exclamation point on the farce.

the captain was glad in his heart because he knew that he had much honour in the eyes of his men because of the bargain that he had made. So the sailors drank the wine of their native land, and soon their thoughts were back in fair Belzoond and the little neighbouring cities of Durl and Duz.

But for me the captain poured into a little jar some heavy yellow wine from a small jar which he kept apart among his sacred things. Thick and sweet it was, even like honey, yet there was in its heart a mighty, ardent fire which had authority over souls of men. It was made, the captain told me, with great subtlety by the secret craft of a family of six who lived in a hut on the mountains of Hian Min. Once in these mountains, he said, he followed the spoor of a bear, and he came suddenly on a man of that family who had hunted the same bear, and he was at the end of a narrow way with precipice all about him, and his spear was sticking in the bear, and the wound was not fatal, and he had no other weapon. And the bear was walking to-wards the man, very slowly because his wound irked him—yet he was now very close. And what he captain did he would not say, but every year as soon as the snows are hard, and travelling is easy on the Hian Min, that man comes down to the market in the plains, and always leaves for the captain in the gate of fair Belzoond a vessel of that priceless secret wine.

And as I sipped the wine and the captain talked, I remembered me of stalwart noble things that I had long since resolutely planned, and my soul seemed to grow mightier within me and to dominate the whole tide of the Yann. It may be that I then slept. Or, if I did not, I do not now minutely recollect every detail of that morning's occupations. Towards evening, I awoke and wishing to see Perdóndaris before we left in the morning, and being unable to wake the captain, I went ashore alone. Certainly Perdóndaris was a powerful city; it was encompassed by a wall of great strength and altitude, having in it hollow ways for troops to walk in, and battlements along it all the way, and fifteen strong towers on it in every mile, and copper plaques low down where men could read them, telling in all the languages of those parts of the earth—one language on each plaque—the tale of how an army once attacked Perdóndaris and what befell that army. Then I entered Perdóndaris and found all the people dancing, clad in brilliant silks, and playing on the tambang as they danced. For a fearful thunderstorm had terrified them while I slept, and the fires of death, they said, had danced over Perdóndaris, and now the thunder had gone leaping away large and black and hideous, they said, over the distant hills, and had turned round snarling at them, shoving his gleaming teeth, and had stamped, as he went, upon the hilltops until they rang as though they had been bronze. And often and again they stopped in their merry dances and prayed to the God they knew not, saying, "O, God that we know not, we thank Thee for sending the thunder back to his hills." And I went on and came to the market-place, and lying there upon the marble pavement I saw the merchant fast asleep and breathing heavily, with his face and the palms of his hands towards the sky, and slaves were fanning him to keep away the flies. And from the market-place I came to a silver temple and then to a palace of onyx, and there were many wonders in Perdóndaris, and I would have stayed and seen them all, but as I came to the outer wall of the city I suddenly saw in it a huge ivory gate[49]. For a while I paused and admired it, then I came nearer and perceived the dreadful truth. The gate was carved out of one solid piece!

I fled at once through the gateway and down to the ship, and even as I ran I thought that I heard far off on the hills behind me the tramp of the fearful beast by whom that mass of ivory was shed, who was perhaps even then looking for his other tusk. When I was on the ship again I felt safer, and I said nothing to the sailors of what I had seen.

---

[49] There is a literary tradition going as far back as The Odyssey that a "gate of ivory" is a gate of false dreams. As we are in the dream lands, this is likely the allusion that Dunsany was going for, painting Perdóndaris as duplicitous and unable to trick the gods by praying to them generically.

And now the captain was gradually awakening. Now night was rolling up from the East and North, and only the pinnacles of the towers of Perdóndaris still took the fallen sunlight. Then I went to the captain and told him quietly of the thing I had seen. And he questioned me at once about the gate, in a low voice, that the sailors might not know; and I told him how the weight of the thing was such that it could not have been brought from afar, and the captain knew that it had not been there a year ago. We agreed that such a beast could never have been killed by any assault of man, and that the gate must have been a fallen tusk, and one fallen near and recently. Therefore he decided that it were better to flee at once; so he commanded, and the sailors went to the sails, and others raised the anchor to the deck, and just as the highest pinnacle of marble lost the last rays of the sun we left Perdóndaris, that famous city. And night came down and cloaked Perdóndaris and hid it from our eyes, which as things have happened will never see it again; for I have heard since that something swift and wonderful has suddenly wrecked Perdóndaris in a day—towers, walls and people.

And the night deepened over the River Yann, a night all white with stars. And with the night there rose the helmsman's song. As soon as he had prayed he began to sing to cheer himself all through the lonely night. But first he prayed, praying the helmsman's prayer. And this is what I remember of it, rendered into English with a very feeble equivalent of the rhythm that seemed so resonant in those tropic nights.

To whatever god may hear.

Wherever there be sailors whether of river or sea: whether their way be dark or whether through storm: whether their peril be of beast or of rock: or from enemy lurking on land or pursuing on sea: wherever the tiller is cold or the helmsman stiff: wherever sailors sleep or helmsmen watch: guard, guide and return us to the old land, that has known us: to the far homes that we know.

To all the gods that are.

To whatever god may hear.[50]

So he prayed, and there was silence. And the sailors laid them down to rest for the night. The silence deepened, and was only broken by the ripples of Yann that lightly touched our prow. Sometimes some monster of the river coughed.

Silence and ripples, ripples and silence again.

And then his loneliness came upon the helmsman, and he began to sing. And he sang the market songs of Durl and Duz, and the old dragon-legends of Belzoond.

---

[50] We can contrast this with the prayer in Perdóndaris. This is a plea to "all the gods" whereas in Perdóndaris they offered thanks to whatever god may have been helping them at the time.

Many a song he sang, telling to spacious and exotic Yann the little tales and trifles of his city of Durl. And the songs welled up over the black jungle and came into the clear cold air above, and the great bands of stars that look on Yann began to know the affairs of Durl and Duz, and of the shepherds that dwelt in the fields between, and the flocks that they had, and the loves that they had loved, and all the little things that they had hoped to do. And as I lay wrapped up in skins and blankets, listening to those songs, and watching the fantastic shapes of the great trees like to black giants stalking through the night, I suddenly fell asleep.

When I awoke great mists were trailing away from the Yann. And the flow of the river was tumbling now tumultuously, and little waves appeared; for Yann had scented from afar the ancient crags of Glorm, and knew that their ravines lay cool before him wherein he should meet the merry wild Irillion rejoicing from fields of snow. So he shook off from him the torpid sleep that had come upon him in the hot and scented jungle, and forgot its orchids and its butterflies, and swept on turbulent, expectant, strong; and soon the snowy peaks of the Hills of Glorm came glittering into view. And now the sailors were waking up from sleep. Soon we all ate, and then the helmsman laid him down to sleep while a comrade took his place, and they all spread over him their choicest furs.

And in a while we heard the sound that the Irillion made as she came down dancing from the fields of snow.

And then we saw the ravine in the Hills of Glorm lying precipitous and smooth before us, into which we were carried by the leaps of Yann. And now we left the steamy jungle and breathed the mountain air; the sailors stood up and took deep breaths of it, and thought of their own far off Acroctian hills on which were Durl and Duz—below them in the plains stands fair Belzoond.

A great shadow brooded between the cliffs of Glorm, but the crags were shining above us like gnarled moons, and almost lit the gloom. Louder and louder came the Irillion's song, and the sound of her dancing down from the fields of snow. And soon we saw her white and full of mists, and wreathed with rainbows delicate and small that she had plucked up near the mountain's summit from some celestial garden of the Sun. Then she went away seawards with the huge grey Yann and the ravine widened, and opened upon the world, and our rocking ship came through to the light of the day.

And all that morning and all the afternoon we passed through the marshes of Pondoovery; and Yann widened there, and flowed solemnly and slowly, and the captain bade the sailors beat on bells to overcome the dreariness of the marshes.

At last the Irusian mountains came in sight, nursing the villages of Pen-Kai and Blut, and the wandering streets of Mlo, where priests propitiate the avalanche with wine and maize. Then night came down over the plains of Tlun, and we saw the lights of Cappadarnia. We heard the Pathnites beating upon drums as we passed Imaut and Golzunda, then all but the helmsman slept. And villages scattered along the banks of the Yann heard all that night in the helmsman's unknown tongue the little songs of cities that they knew not.

I awoke before dawn with a feeling that I was unhappy before I remembered why. Then I recalled that by the evening of the approaching day, according to all foreseen probabilities, we should come to Bar-Wul-Yann, and I should part from the captain and his sailors. And I had liked the man because he had given me of his yellow wine that was set apart among his sacred things, and many a story he had told me about his fair Belzoond between the Acroctian hills and the Hian Min. And I had liked the ways that his sailors had, and the prayers that they prayed at evening side by side, grudging not one another their alien gods. And I had a liking too for the tender way in which they often spoke of Durl and Duz, for it is good that men should love their native cities and the little hills that hold those cities up.

And I had come to know who would meet them when they re-turned to their homes, and where they thought the meetings would take place, some in a valley of the Acroctian hills where the road comes up from Yann, others in the gateway of one or another of the three cities, and others by the fireside in the home. And I thought of the danger that had menaced us all alike outside Perdóndaris, a danger that, as things have happened, was very real.

And I thought too of the helmsman's cheery song in the cold and lonely night, and how he had held our lives in his careful hands[51]. And as I thought of this the helmsman ceased to sing, and I looked up and saw a pale light had appeared in the sky, and the lonely night had passed; and the dawn widened, and the sailors awoke.

And soon we saw the tide of the Sea himself advancing resolute between Yann's borders, and Yann sprang lithely at him and they struggled awhile; then Yann and all that was his were pushed back northward, so that the sailors had to hoist the sails and, the wind being favorable, we still held onwards.

And we passed Gondara and Narl and Haz. And we saw memorable, holy Golnuz, and heard the pilgrims praying.

When we awoke after the midday rest we were coming near to Nen, the last of the cities on the River Yann. And the jungle was all about us once again, and about Nen; but

---

[51] Contrast this with the description of the passing of the night in Bethmoora.

the great Mloon ranges stood up over all things, and watched the city from beyond the jungle.

Here we anchored, and the captain and I went up into the city and found that the Wanderers[52] had come into Nen.

And the Wanderers were a weird, dark, tribe, that once in every seven years came down from the peaks of Mloon, having crossed by a pass that is known to them from some fantastic land that lies beyond. And the people of Nen were all outside their houses, and all stood wondering at their own streets. For the men and women of the Wanderers had crowded all the ways, and every one was doing some strange thing. Some danced astounding dances that they had learned from the desert wind, rapidly curving and swirling till the eye could follow no longer. Others played upon instruments beautiful wailing tunes that were full of horror, which souls had taught them lost by night in the desert, that strange far desert from which the Wanderers came.

None of their instruments were such as were known in Nen nor in any part of the region of the Yann; even the horns out of which some were made were of beasts that none had seen along the river, for they were barbed at the

---

[52] The use of this generic word as proper noun is interesting here, because clearly the poet and the captain are also "wanderers" come to this city, as are we, the readers.

tips. And they sang, in the language of none, songs that seemed to be akin to the mysteries of night and to the unreasoned fear that haunts dark places.

Bitterly all the dogs of Nen distrusted them. And the Wanderers told one another fearful tales, for though no one in Nen knew ought of their language yet they could see the fear on the listeners' faces, and as the tale wound on the whites of their eyes showed vividly in terror as the eyes of some little beast whom the hawk has seized. Then the teller of the tale would smile and stop, and another would tell his story, and the teller of the first tale's lips would chatter with fear. And if some deadly snake chanced to appear the Wanderers would greet him as a brother, and the snake would seem to give his greetings to them before he passed on again. Once that most fierce and lethal of tropic snakes, the giant lythra, came out of the jungle and all down the street, the central street of Nen, and none of the Wanderers moved away from him, but they all played sonorously on drums, as though he had been a person of much honour; and the snake moved through the midst of them and smote none.

Even the Wanderers' children could do strange things, for if any one of them met with a child of Nen the two would stare at each other in silence with large grave eyes; then the Wanderers' child would slowly draw from his turban a live fish or snake. And the children of Nen could do nothing of that kind at all.

Much I should have wished to stay and hear the hymn with which they greet the night, that is answered by the wolves on the heights of Mloon, but it was now time to raise the anchor again that the captain might return from Bar-Wul-Yann upon the landward tide. So we went on board and continued down the Yann. And the captain and I spoke little, for we were thinking of our parting, which should be for long, and we watched instead the splendour of the westerning sun. For the sun was a ruddy gold, but a faint mist cloaked the jungle, lying low, and into it poured the smoke of the little jungle cities, and the smoke of them met together in the mist and joined into one haze, which became purple, and was lit by the sun, as the thoughts of men become hallowed by some great and sacred thing. Some times one column from a lonely house would rise up higher than the cities' smoke, and gleam by itself in the sun.

And now as the sun's last rays were nearly level, we saw the sight that I had come to see, for from two mountains that stood on either shore two cliffs of pink marble came out into the river, all glowing in the light of the low sun, and they were quite smooth and of mountainous altitude, and they nearly met, and Yann went tumbling between them and found the sea.

And this was Bar-Wul-Yann, the Gate of Yann, and in the distance through that barrier's gap I saw the azure indescribable sea, where little fishing-boats went gleaming by.

And the sun set, and the brief twilight came, and the exultation of the glory of Bar-Wul-Yann was gone, yet still the pink cliffs glowed, the fairest marvel that the eye beheld—and this in a land of wonders. And soon the twilight gave place to the coming out of stars, and the colours of Bar-Wul-Yann went dwindling away. And the sight of those cliffs was to me as some chord of music that a master's hand had launched from the violin, and which carries to Heaven or Faëry the tremulous spirits of men.

And now by the shore they anchored and went no further, for they were sailors of the river and not of the sea[53], and knew the Yann but not the tides beyond.

And the time was come when the captain and I must part, he to go back to his fair Belzoond in sight of the distant peaks of the Hian Min, and I to find my way by strange means back to those hazy fields that all poets know, wherein stand small mysterious cottages through whose windows, looking westwards, you may see the

---

[53] The story ends without him getting to the sea. He has traveled all this way only to get close enough to view it from the shore, and the crew of the Bird of Yann can take him no further. If you are reading this piece metaphorically your interpretation probably hinges on how you think of this sentence.

fields of men, and looking eastwards see glittering elfin mountains[54], tipped with snow, going range on range into the region of Myth, and beyond it into the kingdom of Fantasy, which pertain to the Lands of Dream. Long we regarded one another, knowing that we should meet no more, for my fancy is weakening as the years slip by, and I go ever more seldom into the Lands of Dream[55]. Then we clasped hands, uncouthly on his part, for it is not the method of greeting in his country, and he commended my soul to the care of his own gods, to his little lesser gods, the humble ones, to the gods that bless Belzoond[56].

---

[54] This is an idea Dunsany will pick up again and play with in depth in his later novel The King of Elfland's Daughter.

[55] Here is perhaps the heart of the what Dunsany is wrestling with. As time progresses he feels his imagination give way. It's a difficult and sad thing to realize this. Should he try to arrest time? To stop it as those in this story? Or should he simply appreciate the time he has and each of his few remaining days in the Land of Dreams?

[56] "Arguably Dunsany's masterpiece. I love it not only for its effortless invention and beauty but because it so amiably refutes all the Creative Writing Program dogma about 'conflict' and 'plot line' and 'character'" It leaves out all that stuff, setting you adrift on the river of pure story." Ursula K. Le Guin.

The Sword and the Idol

It was a cold winter's evening late in the Stone Age; the sun had gone down blazing over the plains of Thold; there were no clouds, only the chill blue sky and the imminence of stars; and the surface of the sleeping Earth began to harden against the cold of the night. Presently from their lairs arose, and shook themselves and went stealthily forth, those of Earth's children to whom it is the law to prowl abroad as soon as the dusk has fallen. And they went pattering softly over the plain, and their eyes shone in the dark, and crossed and recrossed one another in their courses. Suddenly there became manifest in the midst of the plain that fearful portent of the presence of Man—a little flickering fire. And the children of Earth who prowl abroad by night looked sideways at it and snarled and edged away; all but the wolves, who came a little nearer, for it was winter and the wolves were hungry, and they had come in thousands from the mountains, and they said in their hearts, "We are strong." Around the fire a little tribe was encamped. They, too, had come from the mountains, and from lands beyond them, but it was in the mountains that the wolves first winded them; they picked up bones at first that the tribe had dropped, but they were closer now and on all sides. It was Loz who had lit the fire.

He had killed a small furry beast, hurling his stone axe at it, and had gathered a quantity of reddish-brown stones, and had laid them in a long row, and placed bits of the small beast all along it; then he lit a fire on each side, and the stones heated, and the bits began to cook. It was at this time that the tribe noticed that the wolves who had followed them so far were no longer content with the scraps of deserted encampments. A line of yellow eyes surrounded them, and when it moved it was to come nearer. So the men of the tribe hastily tore up brushwood, and felled a small tree with their flint axes, and heaped it all over the fire that Loz had made, and for a while the great heap hid the flame, and the wolves came trotting in and sat down again on their haunches much closer than before; and the fierce and valiant dogs that belonged to the tribe believed that their end was about to come while fighting, as they had long since prophesied it would. Then the flame caught the lofty stack of brushwood, and rushed out of it, and ran up the side of it, and stood up haughtily far over the top, and the wolves seeing this terrible ally of Man reveling there in his strength, and knowing nothing of this frequent treachery to his masters, went slowly away as though they had other purposes. And for the rest of that night the dogs of the encampment cried out to them and besought them to come back. But the tribe lay down all round the fire under thick furs and slept. And a great wind arose and blew into the roaring heart of the fire till it was red no longer, but all pallid with heat. With the dawn the tribe awoke.

Loz might have known that after such a mighty conflagration nothing could remain of his small furry beast, but there was hunger in him and little reason as he searched among the ashes. What he found there amazed him beyond measure; there was no meat, there was not even his row of reddish-brown stones, but something longer than a man's leg and narrower than his hand, was lying there like a great flattened snake[57]. When Loz looked at its thin edges and saw that it ran to a point, he picked up stones to chip it and make it sharp. It was the instinct of Loz to sharpen things. When he found that it could not be chipped his wonderment increased. It was many hours before he discovered that he could sharpen the edges by rubbing them with a stone; but at last the point was sharp, and all one side of it except near the end, where Loz held it in his hand. And Loz lifted it and brandished it, and the Stone Age was over. That afternoon in the little encampment, just as the tribe moved on, the Stone Age passed away, which, for perhaps thirty or forty thousand years,

---

[57] Dunsany has to make this a spectacular campfire because campfires are usually about 200 °C too cold to melt copper. It's theorized that the discovery of copperworking came from it being melted in pottery kilns.

had slowly lifted Man from among the beasts and left him with his supremacy beyond all hope of reconquest.

It was not for many days that any other man tried to make for him-self an iron sword[58] by cooking the same kind of small furry beast that Loz had tried to cook. It was not for many years that any thought to lay the meat along stones as Loz had done; and when they did, being no longer on the plains of Thold, they used flints or chalk. It was not for many generations that another piece of iron ore was melted and the secret slowly guessed. Nevertheless one of Earth's many veils was torn aside by Loz to give us ultimately the steel sword and the plough, machinery and factories; let us not blame Loz if we think that he did wrong, for he did all in ignorance. The tribe moved on until it came to water, and there it settled down under a hill, and they built their huts there. Very soon they had to fight with another tribe, a tribe that was stronger than they; but the sword of Loz was terrible and his tribe slew their foes. You might make one blow at Loz, but then would come one thrust from that iron sword, and there

---

[58] This is a liberty of Dunsany's. It is impossible that Dunsany didn't know that copper and bronze working came before iron working and that iron is substantially harder to smelt than copper. There is no way that iron ore could melt in a campfire. But I believe for Dunsany the iron sword is a more romantic image and one that would be more evocative of war ("Blood and Iron") to his modern audience.

was no way of surviving it. No one could fight with Loz. And he became ruler of the tribe in the place of Iz, who hitherto had ruled it with his sharp axe, as his father had before him.

Now Loz begat Lo, and in his old age gave his sword to him, and Lo ruled the tribe with it. And Lo called the name of the sword Death, because it was so swift and terrible.

And Iz begat Ird, who was of no account. And Ird hated Lo because he was of no account by reason of the iron sword of Lo.[59]

One night Ird stole down to the hut of Lo, carrying his sharp axe, and he went very softly, but Lo's dog, Warner, heard him coming, and he growled softly by his master's door. When Ird came to the hut he heard Lo talking gently to his sword. And Lo was saying, "Lie still, Death. Rest, rest, old sword," and then, "What, again, Death? Be still. Be still."

And then again: "What, art thou hungry, Death? Or thirsty, poor old sword?

Soon, Death, soon. Be still only a little."

But Ird fled, for he did not like the gentle tone of Lo as he spoke to his sword.

---

[59] These two paragraphs are very biblical in construction and are very clearly inspired by one of Dunsany's biggest stylistic inspirations: the King James bible.

And Lo begat Lod. And when Lo died Lod took the iron sword and ruled the tribe.

And Ird begat Ith, who was of no account, like his father.

Now when Lod had smitten a man or killed a terrible beast, Ith would go away for a while into the forest rather than hear the praises that would be given to Lod.

And once, as Ith sat in the forest waiting for the day to pass, he suddenly thought he saw a tree trunk looking at him as with a face. And Ith was afraid, for trees should not look at men. But soon Ith saw that it was only a tree and not a man, though it was like a man. Ith used to speak to this tree, and tell it about Lod, for he dared not speak to any one else about him. And Ith found comfort in speaking about Lod.

One day Ith went with his stone axe into the forest, and stayed there many days.

He came back by night, and the next morning when the tribe awoke they saw something that was like a man and yet was not a man. And it sat on the hill with its elbows pointing outwards and was quite still. And Ith was crouching before it, and hurriedly placing before it fruits and flesh, and then leaping away from it and looking frightened. Presently all the tribe came out to see, but dared not come quite close because of the fear that they saw on the face of Ith. And Ith went to his hut, and came back again with a hunting spear-head and valuable small stone knives, and reached out and laid them before the thing that was like a man, and then sprang away from it.

And some of the tribe questioned Ith about the still thing that was like a man, and Ith said, "This is Ged." Then they asked, "Who is Ged?" and Ith said, "Ged sends the crops and the rain; and the sun and the moon are Ged's[60]."

Then the tribe went back to their huts, but later in the day some came again, and they said to Ith, "Ged is only as we are, having hands and feet." And Ith pointed to the right hand of Ged, which was not as his left, but was shaped like the paw of a beast, and Ith said, "By this ye may know that he is not as any man."

Then they said, "He is indeed Ged." But Lod said, "He speaketh not, nor doth he eat," and Ith answered, "The thunder is his voice and the famine is his eating."[61]

---

[60] A not very subtle play on the word "God".

[61] In Idle Days on the Yann Dunsany played with many different possibilities for how humanity would deal with gods in a context where the reader was supposed to believe they were real. Here Dunsany creates a single false god and lets the reader know it is false before exploring its effect on humanity. Interestingly Dunsany's many "real" gods occur in a fantasy setting while his one false god is set in a story that's supposed to be part of the world we live in, perhaps giving us an insight into some of the questions he was wrestling with at the time.

After this the tribe copied Ith, and brought little gifts of meat to Ged; and Ith cooked them before him that Ged might smell the cooking.

One day a great thunderstorm came trampling up from the distance and raged among the hills, and the tribe all hid away from it in their huts. And Ith appeared among the huts looking unafraid. And Ith said little, but the tribe thought that he had expected the terrible storm because the meat that they had laid before Ged had been tough meat, and not the best parts of the beasts they slew.

And Ged grew to have more honour among the tribe than Lod. And Lod was vexed.

One night Lod arose when all were asleep, and quieted his dog, and took his iron sword and went away to the hill. And he came on Ged in the starlight, sitting still, with his elbows pointing outwards, and his beast's paw, and the mark of the fire on the ground where his food had been cooked.

And Lod stood there for a while in great fear, trying to keep to his purpose. Suddenly he stepped up close to Ged and lifted his iron sword, and Ged neither hit nor shrank. Then the thought came into Lod's mind, "Ged does not hit. What will Ged do instead?"

And Lod lowered his sword and struck not, and his imagination began to work on that "What will Ged do instead?"

And the more Lod thought, the worse was his fear of Ged.

And Lod ran away and left him.

Lod still ruled the tribe in battle or in the hunt, but the chiefest spoils of battle were given to Ged, and the beasts that they slew were Ged's; and all questions that concerned war or peace, and questions of law and disputes, were always brought to him, and Ith gave the answers after speaking to Ged by night.

At last Ith said, the day after an eclipse, that the gifts which they brought to Ged were not enough, that some far greater sacrifice was needed, that Ged was very angry even now, and not to be appeased by any ordinary sacrifice.

And Ith said that to save the tribe from the anger of Ged he would speak to Ged that night, and ask him what new sacrifice he needed.

Deep in his heart Lod shuddered, for his instinct told him that Ged wanted

Lod's only son, who should hold the iron sword when Lod was gone.

No one would dare touch Lod because of the iron sword, but his instinct said in his slow mind again and again, "Ged loves Ith. Ith has said so. Ith hates the sword-holders."

"Ith hates the sword-holders. Ged loves Ith."

Evening fell and the night came when Ith should speak with Ged, and Lod became ever surer of the doom of his race.

He lay down but could not sleep.

Midnight had barely come when Lod arose and went with his iron sword again to the hill.

And there sat Ged. Had Ith been to him yet? Ith whom Ged loved, who hated the sword-holders.

And Lod looked long at the old sword of iron that had come to his grandfather on the plains of Thold.

Good-bye, old sword! And Lod laid it on the knees of Ged, then went away.

And when Ith came, a little before dawn, the sacrifice was found acceptable unto Ged[62].

---

[62] Interestingly in the end this becomes a "swords to plowshares" parable. While most of the tale is about trickery and revenge, about false gods and spiritual vs temporal power Dunsany gives us a subtle perspective on these question by concluding by having the sword "Death" sacrificed to the idol of rain and harvest. Maybe it doesn't matter that it's a false idol? Maybe it's effect is all that matters? These questions may also have taken on whole new dimensions for a man who saw the world on the path to the First World War.

The Idle City[63]

There was once a city which was an idle city, wherein men told vain tales.

And it was that city's custom to tax all men that would enter in, with the toll of some idle story in the gate.

So all men paid to the watchers in the gate the toll of an idle story, and passed into the city unhindered and un-hurt. And in a certain hour of the night when the king of that city arose and went pacing swiftly up and down the chamber of his sleeping, and called upon the name of the dead queen, then would the watchers fasten up the gate and go into that chamber to the king, and, sitting on the floor, would tell him all the tales that they had gathered. And listening to them some calmer mood would come upon the king, and listening still he would lie down again and at last fall asleep, and all the watchers silently would arise and steal away from the chamber[64].

A while ago wandering, I came to the gate of that city. And even as I came a man stood up to pay his toll to the

---

[63] In Dunsany's characteristic word play, this is the third story in a row whose title involves either Idle or Idol.

[64] Sir Richard Burton, the translator of the Arabian Nights was the cousin of Dunsany's mother and it is from his translation that Dunsany appears to have drawn some of the inspiration for this piece.

watchers. They were seated cross-legged on the ground between him and the gate, and each one held a spear. Near him two other travelers sat on the warm sand waiting. And the man said:

"Now the city of Nombros forsook the worship of the gods and turned towards God. So the gods threw their cloaks over their faces and strode away from the city, and going into the haze among the hills passed through the trunks of the olive groves into the sunset. But when they had already left the Earth, they turned and looked through the gleaming folds of the twilight for the last time at their city; and they looked half in anger and half in regret, then turned and went away for ever. But they sent back a Death, who bore a scythe, saying to it: 'Slay half in the city that forsook us, but half of them spare alive that they may yet remember their old forsaken gods.'

"But God sent a destroying angel to show that He was God, saying unto him: 'Go into that city and slay half of the dwellers therein, yet spare a half of them that they may know that I am God.'

"And at once the destroying angel put his hand to his sword, and the sword came out of the scabbard with a deep breath, like to the breath that a broad woodman takes before his first blow at some giant oak. Thereat the angel pointed his arms downwards, and bending his head between them, fell forward from Heaven's edge, and the spring of his ankles shot him downwards with his wings furled behind him. So he went slanting earthward through the evening with his sword stretched out before him, and he was like a javelin that some hunter hath hurled that returneth again to the earth: but just before he touched it he lifted his head and spread his wings with the under feathers forward, and alighted by the bank of the broad Flavro that divides the city of Nombros. And down the bank of the Flavro he fluttered low, like to a hawk over a new-cut cornfield when the little creatures of the corn are shelterless, and at the same time down the other bank the Death from the gods went mowing.

"At once they saw each other, and the angel glared at the Death, and the Death leered back at him, and the flames in the eyes of the angel illumined with a red glare the mist that lay in the hollows of the sockets of the Death. Suddenly they fell on one another, sword to scythe. And the angel captured the temples of the gods, and set up over them the sign of God, and the Death captured the temples of God, and led into them the ceremonies and sacrifices of the gods; and all the while the centuries slipped quietly by, going down the Flavro seawards.

"And now some worship God in the temple of the gods, and others worship the gods in the temple of God, and still the angel hath not returned again to the rejoicing choirs, and still the Death hath not gone back to die with the dead gods; but all through Nombros they fight up and down, and still on each side of the Flavro the city lives."

And the watchers in the gate said, "Enter in.[65]"

Then another traveler rose up, and said:

"Solemnly between Huhenwazy and Nitcrana the huge grey clouds came floating. And those great mountains, heavenly Huhenwazi and Nitcrana, the king of peaks, greeted them, calling them brothers. And the clouds were glad of their greeting, for they meet with companions seldom in the lonely heights of the sky.

"But the vapours of evening said unto the earth-mist, 'What are those shapes that dare to move above us and to go where Nitcrana is and Huhenwazi?'

"And the earth-mist said in answer unto the vapours of evening, 'It is only an earth-mist that has become mad and has left the warm and comfortable earth, and has in his madness thought that his place is with Huhenwazi and Nitcrana.'

"'Once,' said the vapours of evening, 'there were clouds, but this was many and many a day ago, as our forefathers have said. Perhaps the mad one thinks he is the clouds.'

"Then spake the earth-worms from the warm deeps of the mud, saying 'O earth-mist, thou art indeed the

---

[65] This formulation lets Dunsany tell a number of shorter short stories within this tale, but he links them all by making them follow the same rules of form and theme. Each is a story about a place that concludes with a mini-parable in the last sentence or paragraph.

clouds, and there are no clouds but thou. And as for Huhenwazi and Nitcrana, I cannot see them, and therefore they are not high, and there are no mountains in the world but those that I cast up every morning out of the deeps of the mud.'

"And the earth-mist and the vapours of evening were glad at the voice of the earth-worms, and looking earthward believed what they had said.

"And indeed it is better to be as the earth-mist, and to keep close to the warm mud at night, and to hear the earth-worm's comfortable speech, and not to be a wanderer in the cheerless heights, but to leave the mountains alone with their desolate snow, to draw what comfort they can from their vast aspect over all the cities of men, and from the whispers that they hear at evening of unknown distant gods."

And the watchers in the gate said, "Enter in."

Then a man stood up who came out of the west, and told a western tale. He said:

"There is a road in Rome[66] that runs through an ancient temple that once the gods had loved; it runs along

---

[66] Once again Dunsany blurs the line between our world and the world of the fantastic, much in the way it can become blurred in dreams. His worlds almost always meet in the more mythological parts of our realm, such as here with Rome, seat of empires and popes, where making miracles commonplace seems reasonable.

the top of a great wall, and the floor of the temple lies far down beneath it, of marble, pink and white.

"Upon the temple floor I counted to the number of thirteen hungry cats.

"'Sometimes,' they said among themselves, 'it was the gods that lived here, sometimes it was men, and now it's cats. So let us enjoy the sun on the hot marble before another people comes.'

"For it was at that hour of a warm afternoon when my fancy is able to hear silent voices.

"And the awful leanness of all those thirteen cats moved me to go into a neighbouring fish shop, and there to buy a quantity of fishes. Then I returned and threw them all over the railing at the top of the great wall, and they fell for thirty feet, and hit the sacred marble with a smack.

"Now, in any other town but Rome, or in the minds of any other cats, the sight of fishes falling out of heaven had surely excited wonder. They rose slowly, and all stretched themselves, then they came leisurely towards the fishes. 'It is only a miracle,' they said in their hearts."

And the watchers in the gate said, "Enter in."

Proudly and slowly, as they spoke, drew up to them a camel, whose rider sought entrance to the city. His face shone with the sunset by which for long he had steered for the city's gate. Of him they demanded toll. Whereat he spoke to his camel, and the camel roared and kneeled, and the man descended from him. And the man unwrapped from many silks a box of divers metals wrought by the Japanese, and on the lid of it were figures of men who gazed from some shore at an isle of the Inland Sea. This he showed to the watchers, and when they had seen it, said, "It has seemed to me that these speak to each other thus:

"'Behold now Oojni[67], the dear one of the sea, the little mother sea that hath no storms. She goeth out from Oojni singing a song, and she returneth singing over her sands. Little is Oojni in the lap of the sea, and scarce to be perceived by wondering ships. White sails have never wafted her legends afar, they are told not by bearded wanderers of the sea. Her fireside tales are known not to the North, the dragons of China have not heard of them, nor those that ride on elephants through Ind.

"'Men tell the tales and the smoke ariseth upwards; the smoke departeth and the tales are told.

"'Oojni is not a name among the nations, she is not known of where the merchants meet, she is not spoken of by alien lips.

"'Indeed, but Oojni is a little among the isles, yet is she loved by those that know her coasts and her inland places hidden from the sea.

---

[67] No such sea exists, but it is possible that he is drawing from tales of the Seto Inland Sea to create this mythological waterway.

"Without glory, without fame, and without wealth, Oojni is greatly loved by a little people, and by a few; yet not by few, for all her dead still love her, and oft by night come whispering through her woods. Who could forget Oojni even among the dead?

"For here in Oojni, wot you, are homes of men, and gardens, and golden temples of the gods, and sacred places inshore from the sea, and many murmurous woods. And there is a path that winds over the hills to go into mysterious holy lands where dance by night the spirits of the woods, or sing unseen in the sunlight; and no one goes into these holy lands, for who that love Oojni could rob her of her mysteries, and the curious aliens come not. Indeed, but we love Oojni though she is so little; she is the little mother of our race, and the kindly nurse of all seafaring birds.

"And behold, even now caressing her, the gentle fingers of the mother sea, whose dreams are far with that old wanderer Ocean.

"And yet let us forget not Fuzi-Yama[68], for he stands manifest over clouds and sea, misty below, and vague and indistinct, but clear above for all the isles to watch. The ships make all their journeys in his sight, the nights and the days go by him like a wind, the summers and winters

---

[68] This is an archaic spelling of Fuji-Yama or Mount Fuji in central Japan.

under him flicker and fade, the lives of men pass quietly here and hence, and Fuzi-Yama watches there—and knows."

And the watchers in the gate said, "Enter in."

And I, too, would have told them a tale, very wonderful and very true; one that I had told in many cities, which as yet had no believers. But now the sun had set, and the brief twilight gone, and ghostly silences were rising from far and darkening hills. A stillness hung over that city's gate. And the great silence of the solemn night was more acceptable to the watchers in the gate than any sound of man. There-fore they beckoned to us, and motioned with their hands that we should pass untaxed into the city. And softly we went up over the sand, and between the high rock pillars of the gate, and a deep stillness settled among the watchers, and the stars over them twinkled undisturbed.

For how short a while man speaks, and withal how vainly. And for how long he is silent. Only the other day I met a king in Thebes, who had been silent already for four thousand years[69].

---

[69] This is probably him reading Oedipus. Once again Dunsany is playing with themes of time, aging and dying, but here by bringing in the Oedipus reference he forces us to question his own question. By telling stories isn't Oedipus still speaking after all these years?

The Hashish Man

I was at a dinner in London the other day. The ladies had gone up-stairs, and no one sat on my right; on my left there was a man I did not know, but he knew my name somehow apparently, for he turned to me after a while, and said, "I read a story of yours about Bethmoora in a review."[70]

Of course I remembered the tale. It was about a beautiful Oriental city that was suddenly deserted in a day—nobody quite knew why. I said, "Oh, yes," and slowly searched in my mind for some more fitting acknowledgment of the compliment that his memory had paid me.

I was greatly astonished when he said, "You were wrong about the gnousar sickness; it was not that at all."

I said, "Why! Have you been there?"

And he said, "Yes; I do it with hashish. I know Bethmoora well." And he took out of his pocket a small box full of some black stuff that looked like tar, but had a

---

[70] This is the first time we get confirmation that the stories told in the first person here are also supposed to be the author (or a fictionalized version of him).

stranger smell. He warned me not to touch it with my finger, as the stain remained for days. "I got it from a gipsy," he said. "He had a lot of it, as it had killed his father[71]." But I interrupted him, for I wanted to know for certain what it was that had made desolate that beautiful city, Bethmoora, and why they fled from it swiftly in a day. "Was it because of the Desert's curse?" I asked. And he said, "Partly it was the fury of the Desert and partly the advice of the Emperor Thuba Mleen, for that fearful beast is in some way connected with the Desert on his mother's side." And he told me this strange story: "You remember the sailor with the black scar, who was there on the day that you described when the messengers came on mules to the gate of Bethmoora, and all the people fled. I met this man in a tavern, drinking rum, and he told me all about the flight from Bethmoora, but knew no more than you did what the message was, or who had sent it. However, he said he would see Bethmoora once more whenever he touched again at an eastern port, even if he had to face the Devil. He often said that he would face the Devil to find out the mystery of that message that emptied Bethmoora in a day. And in the end he had to face Thuba

---

[71] There was by this point a long-standing tradition in "orientalist" stories to use opium to introduce the fantastic. I suspect Dunsany is using hashish as a stand in for opium because opium was becoming cliché (but truly using it as a stand in without really changing any of its properties).

Mleen, whose weak ferocity he had not imagined. For one day the sailor told me he had found a ship, and I met him no more after that in the tavern drinking rum. It was about that time that I got the hashish from the gipsy, who had a quantity that he did not want. It takes one literally out of oneself. It is like wings. You swoop over distant countries and into other worlds. Once I found out the secret of the universe. I have forgotten what it was, but I know that the Creator does not take Creation seriously, for I remember that He sat in Space with all His work in front of Him and laughed. I have seen incredible things in fearful worlds. As it is your imagination that takes you there, so it is only by your imagination that you can get back. Once out in aether I met a battered, prowling spirit, that had belonged to a man whom drugs had killed a hundred years ago; and he led me to regions that I had never imagined; and we parted in anger beyond the Pleiades, and I could not imagine my way back[72]. And I met a huge grey shape that was the Spirit of some great people, perhaps of a whole star, and I besought It to show me my way home, and It halted beside me like a sudden wind and pointed, and, speaking quite softly, asked me if I discerned a certain tiny light, and I saw a far star faintly, and then It said to me, 'That is the Solar System,' and strode tremendously on. And somehow

---

[72] This is somewhat ironic for a sailor as the Pleiades are some of the stars most associated with navigation.

I imagined my way back, and only just in time, for my body was already stiffening in a chair in my room; and the fire had gone out and everything was cold, and I had to move each finger one by one, and there were pins and needles in them, and dreadful pains in the nails, which began to thaw; and at last I could move one arm, and reached a bell, and for a long time no one came, because every one was in bed. But at last a man appeared, and they got a doctor; and HE said that it was hashish poisoning, but it would have been all right if I hadn't met that battered, prowling spirit.

"I could tell you astounding things that I have seen, but you want to know who sent that message to Beth-moora. Well, it was Thuba Mleen. And this is how I know. I often went to the city after that day you wrote of (I used to take hashish of an evening in my flat), and I always found it uninhabited. Sand had poured into it from the desert, and the streets were yellow and smooth, and through open, swinging doors the sand had drifted.

"One evening I had put the guard in front of the fire, and settled into a chair and eaten my hashish, and the first thing that I saw when I came to Bethmoora was the sailor with the black scar, strolling down the street, and making footprints in the yellow sand. And now I knew that I should see what secret power it was that kept Bethmoora uninhabited.

"I saw that there was anger in the Desert, for there were storm clouds heaving along the skyline, and I heard a muttering amongst the sand.

"The sailor strolled on down the street, looking into the empty houses as he went; sometimes he shouted and sometimes he sang, and sometimes he wrote his name on a marble wall. Then he sat down on a step and ate his dinner. After a while he grew tired of the city, and came back up the street. As he reached the gate of green copper three men on camels appeared.

"I could do nothing. I was only a consciousness, invisible, wandering: my body was in Europe. The sailor fought well with his fists, but he was over-powered and bound with ropes, and led away through the Desert.

"I followed for as long as I could stay, and found that they were going by the way of the Desert round the Hills of Hap towards Utnar Véhi, and then I knew that the camel men belonged to Thuba Mleen.

"I work in an insurance office all day, and I hope you won't forget me if ever you want to insure—life, fire, or motor—but that's no part of my story. I was desperately anxious to get back to my flat, though it is not good to take hashish two days running; but I wanted to see what they would do to the poor fellow, for I had heard bad rumours about Thuba Mleen. When at last I got away I had a letter to write; then I rang for my servant, and told him

that I must not be disturbed, though I left my door un-
locked in case of accidents. After that I made up a good
fire, and sat down and partook of the pot of dreams. I was
going to the palace of Thuba Mleen.

"I was kept back longer than usual by noises in the
street, but suddenly I was up above the town; the European countries rushed by beneath me, and there appeared
the thin white palace spires of horrible Thuba Mleen. I
found him presently at the end of a little narrow room. A
curtain of red leather hung behind him, on which all the
names of God, written in Yannish[73], were worked with a
golden thread. Three windows were small and high. The
Emperor seemed no more than about twenty, and looked
small and weak. No smiles came on his nasty yellow face,
though he tittered continually. As I looked from his low
forehead to his quivering under lip, I became aware that
there was some horror about him, though I was not able
to perceive what it was. And then I saw it—the man never
blinked; and though later on I watched those eyes for a
blink, it never happened once.

"And then I followed the Emperor's rapt glance, and
I saw the sail-or lying on the floor, alive but hideously rent,
and the royal torturers were at work all round him. They
had torn long strips from him, but had not detached them,

---

[73] Once again establishing the connection between *Bethmoora* and *Idle
Days on the Yann*

and they were torturing the ends of them far away from the sailor." The man that I met at dinner told me many things which I must omit. "The sailor was groaning softly, and every time he groaned Thuba Mleen tittered. I had no sense of smell, but I could hear and see, and I do not know which was the most revolting—the terrible condition of the sailor or the happy unblinking face of horrible Thuba Mleen.

"I wanted to go away, but the time was not yet come, and I had to stay where I was.

"Suddenly the Emperor's face began to twitch violently and his un-der lip quivered faster, and he whimpered with anger, and cried with a shrill voice, in Yannish, to the captain of his torturers that there was a spirit in the room. I feared not, for living men cannot lay hands on a spirit, but all the torturers were appalled at his anger, and stopped their work, for their hands trembled in fear. Then two men of the spear-guard slipped from the room, and each of them brought back presently a golden bowl, with knobs on it, full of hashish; and the bowls were large enough for heads to have floated in had they been filled with blood. And the two men fell to rapidly, each eating with two great spoons—there was enough in each spoonful to have given dreams to a hundred men. And there came upon them soon the hashish state, and their spirits hovered, preparing to go free, while I feared horribly, but ever and anon they fell back again to their bodies, recalled by some noise in the room. Still the men ate, but lazily now, and without ferocity. At last the great spoons dropped out of their hands, and their spirits rose and left them. I could not flee. And the spirits were more horrible than the men, because they were young men, and not yet wholly moulded to fit their fearful souls. Still the sailor groaned softly, evoking little titters from the Emperor Thuba Mleen. Then the two spirits rushed at me, and swept me thence as gusts of wind sweep butterflies, and away we went from that small, pale, heinous man. There was no escaping from these spirits' fierce insistence. The energy in my minute lump of the drug was overwhelmed by the huge spoonsful that these men had eaten with both hands. I was whirled over Arvle Woondery, and brought to the lands of Snith, and swept on still until I came to Kragua, and beyond this to those bleak lands that are nearly unknown to fancy. And we came at last to those ivory hills that are named the Mountains of Madness[74], and I tried to struggle against the spirits of that frightful Emperor's men, for I heard on the other side of the ivory hills the pittering of those beasts that prey on the mad, as they prowled up and down. It was no fault of mine that my little lump of hashish could not fight with their horrible spoonsful...."

---

[74] It is from this line that H.P. Lovecraft got the name for his famous story *At the Mountains of Madness*.

Some one was tugging at the hall-door bell. Presently a servant came and told our host that a policeman in the hall wished to speak to him at once. He apologized to us, and went outside, and we heard a man in heavy boots, who spoke in a low voice to him. My friend got up and walked over to the window, and opened it, and looked outside. "I should think it will be a fine night," he said. Then he jumped out. When we put our astonished heads out of the window to look for him, he was already out of sight.

Poor Old Bill

On an antique haunt of sailors, a tavern of the sea, the light of day was fading. For several evenings I had frequented this place, in the hope of hearing something from the sailors, as they sat over strange wines, about a rumour that had reached my ears of a certain fleet of galleons of old Spain still said to be afloat in the South Seas in some uncharted region.

In this I was again to be disappointed. Talk was low and seldom, and I was about to leave, when a sailor, wearing ear-rings of pure gold, lifted up his head from his wine, and looking straight before him at the wall, told his tale loudly:

(When later on a storm of rain arose and thundered on the tavern's leaded panes, he raised his voice without effort and spoke on still. The darker it got the clearer his wild eyes[75] shone.)

"A ship with sails of the olden time was nearing fantastic isles. We had never seen such isles.

---

[75] This tale shares much with *The Rime of the Ancient Mariner*. That poem continually refers to its cursed survivor as having "glittering" or "bright" eyes. It seems likely that this is a nod Coleridge's work.

"We all hated the captain, and he hated us. He hated us all alike, there was no favouritism about him. And he never would talk a word with any of us, except sometimes in the evening when it was getting dark he would stop and look up and talk a bit to the men he had hanged at the yard-arm.

"We were a mutinous crew. But Captain was the only man that had pistols. He slept with one under his pillow and kept one close beside him. There was a nasty look about the isles. They were small and flat as though they had come up only recently from the sea, and they had no sand or rocks like honest isles, but green grass down to the water. And there were little cottages there whose looks we did not like. Their thatches came almost down to the ground, and were strangely turned up at the corners, and under the low eaves were queer dark windows whose little leaded[76] panes were too thick to see through. And no one, man or beast, was walking about, so that you could not know what kind of people lived there. But Captain knew. And he went ashore and into one of the cottages, and someone lit lights inside, and the little windows wore an evil look.

"It was quite dark when he came aboard again, and he bade a cheery good-night to the men that swung from the

---

[76] Leadlight windows are akin to stained glass windows, so he probably means these are literally dark, not clear, windows.

yard-arm and he eyed us in a way that frightened poor old Bill.

"Next night we found that he had learned to curse, for he came on a lot of us asleep in our bunks, and among them poor old Bill, and he pointed at us with a finger, and made a curse that our souls should stay all night at the top of the masts. And suddenly there was the soul of poor old Bill sitting like a monkey at the top of the mast, and looking at the stars, and freezing through and through.

"We got up a little mutiny after that, but Captain comes up and points with his finger again, and this time poor old Bill and all the rest are swimming behind the ship through the cold green water, though their bodies remain on deck.

"It was the cabin-boy who found out that Captain couldn't curse when he was drunk, though he could shoot as well at one time as another.

"After that it was only a matter of waiting, and of losing two men when the time came. Some of us were murderous fellows, and wanted to kill Captain, but poor old Bill was for finding a bit of an island, out of the track of ships, and leaving him there with his share of our year's provisions. And everybody listened to poor old Bill, and we decided to maroon Captain as soon as we caught him when he couldn't curse.

"It was three whole days before Captain got drunk again, and poor old Bill and all had a dreadful time, for

Captain invented new curses every day, and wherever he pointed his finger our souls had to go; and the fishes got to know us, and so did the stars, and none of them pitied us when we froze on the masts or were hurried through forests of seaweed and lost our way—both stars and fishes went about their businesses with cold, unastonished eyes. Once when the sun had set and it was twilight, and the moon was showing clearer and clearer in the sky, and we stopped our work for a moment because Captain seemed to be looking away from us at the colours in the sky, he suddenly turned and sent our souls to the Moon. And it was colder there than ice at night; and there were horrible mountains making shadows; and it was all as silent as miles of tombs; and Earth was shining up in the sky as big as the blade of a scythe, and we all got homesick for it, but could not speak nor cry[77]. It was quite dark when we got back, and we were very respectful to Captain all the next day, but he cursed several of us again very soon. What we all feared most was that he would curse our souls to Hell, and none of us mentioned Hell above a whisper for fear that it should remind him. But on the third evening the cabin-boy came and told us that Captain was drunk. And

---

[77] A fairly well research description of a view from the moon for more than a half century before the first person set foot on the moon.

we all went to his cabin, and we found him lying there across his bunk, and he shot as he had never shot before; but he had no more than the two pistols, and he would only have killed two men if he hadn't caught Joe over the head with the end of one of his pistols. And then we tied him up. And poor old Bill put the rum between the Captain's teeth, and kept him drunk for two days, so that he could not curse, till we found a convenient rock. And before sunset of the second day we found a nice bare island for Captain, out of the track of ships, about a hundred yards long and about eighty wide; and we rowed him along to it in a little boat, and gave him provisions for a year, the same as we had ourselves, because poor old Bill wanted to be fair[78]. And we left him sitting comfortable with his back to a rock singing a sailor's song.

"When we could no longer hear Captain singing we all grew very cheerful and made a banquet out of our year's provisions, as we all hoped to be home again in under three weeks. We had three great banquets every day for a week—every man had more than he could eat, and what

---

[78] Marooning was actually considered one of the worst punishments, often worse than execution as the marooned was expected to die slowly of exposure, hunger or thirst. In fact when a crew wanted to be merciful marooned individuals were given a pistol with one shot in it so that they could take their own lives rather than face the slow death of marooning.

was left over we threw on the floor like gentlemen. And then one day, as we saw San Huëgédos[79], and wanted to sail in to spend our money, the wind changed round from behind us and beat us out to sea. There was no tacking against it, and no getting into the harbour, though other ships sailed by us and anchored there. Some-times a dead calm would fall on us, while fishing boats all around us flew before half a gale, and sometimes the wind would beat us out to sea when nothing else was moving. All day we tried, and at night we laid to and tried again the next day. And all the sailors of the other ships were spending their money in San Huëgédos and we could not come nigh it. Then we spoke horrible things against the wind and against San Huëgédos, and sailed away.

"It was just the same at Norenna.

"We kept close together now and talked in low voices. Suddenly poor old Bill grew frightened. As we went all along the Siractic coast-line, we tried again and again, and the wind was waiting for us in every harbour and sent us out to sea. Even the little islands would not have us. And then we knew that there was no landing yet for poor old Bill, and every one upbraided his kind heart that had made them maroon Captain on a rock, so as not to have his blood upon their heads. There was nothing to do but to

---

[79] An invention of Dunsany's, as are all the upcoming place names.

111

drift about the seas. There were no banquets now, because we feared that Captain might live his year and keep us out to sea.

"At first we used to hail all passing ships, and used to try to board them in the boats; but there was no towing against Captain's curse, and we had to give that up. So we played cards for a year in Captain's cabin, night and day, storm and fine, and every one promised to pay poor old Bill when we got ashore.

"It was horrible to us to think what a frugal man Captain really was, he that used to get drunk every other day whenever he was at sea, and here he was still alive, and sober too, for his curse still kept us out of every port, and our provisions were gone.

"Well, it came to drawing lots, and Jim was the unlucky one. Jim only kept us about three days, and then we drew lots again, and this time it was the nigger[80]. The nigger didn't keep us any longer, and we drew again, and this time it was Charlie, and still Captain was alive.

"As we got fewer one of us kept us longer. Longer and longer a mate used to last us, and we all wondered how

---

[80] Not only is Dunsany's use of this word here dehumanizing, but the black character is literally the only one of the entire crew who doesn't get a name. This type of casual racism will play out in later works of fantasy and horror, being made fully explicit by authors like H.P. Lovecraft and even subtly finding its way into the works of Tolkien with the Orcs and Haradrim.

ever Captain did it. It was five weeks over the year when we drew Mike, and he kept us for a week, and Captain was still alive. We wondered he didn't get tired of the same old curse; but we supposed things looked different when one is alone on an island.

"When there was only Jakes and poor old Bill and the cabin-boy and Dick, we didn't draw any longer. We said that the cabin-boy had had all the luck, and he mustn't expect any more. Then poor old Bill was alone with Jakes and Dick, and Captain was still alive. When there was no more boy, and the Captain still alive, Dick, who was a huge strong man like poor old Bill, said that it was Jakes' turn, and he was very lucky to have lived as long as he had. But poor old Bill talked it all over with Jakes, and they thought it better than Dick should take his turn.

"Then there was Jakes and poor old Bill; and Captain would not die.

"And these two used to watch one another night and day, when Dick was gone and no one else was left to them. And at last poor old Bill fell down in a faint and lay there for an hour. Then Jakes came up to him slowly with his knife, and makes a stab at poor old Bill as he lies there on the deck. And poor old Bill caught hold of him by the wrist, and put his knife into him twice to make quite sure, although it spoiled the best part of the meat. Then poor old Bill was all alone at sea[81].

"And the very next week, before the food gave out, Captain must have died on his bit of an island; for poor old Bill heard the Captain's soul going cursing over the sea, and the day after that the ship was cast on a rocky coast.

"And Captain's been dead now for over a hundred years, and poor old Bill is safe ashore again. But it looks as if Captain hadn't done with him yet, for poor old Bill doesn't ever get any older, and somehow or other he doesn't seem to die. Poor old Bill!"

When this was over the man's fascination suddenly snapped, and we all jumped up and left him.

It was not only his revolting story, but it was the fearful look in the eyes of the man who told it, and the terrible ease with which his voice surpassed the roar of the rain, that decided me never again to enter that haunt of sailors—the tavern of the sea.

---

[81] The storyteller *is* "poor old Bill" since no one else would know these details.

The Beggars

I was walking down Piccadilly[82] not long ago, thinking of nursery rhymes and regretting old romance.

As I saw the shopkeepers walk by in their black frock-coats and their black hats, I thought of the old line in nursery annals: "The merchants of London, they wear scarlet." [83]

The streets were all so unromantic, dreary. Nothing could be done for them, I thought—nothing. And then my thoughts were interrupted by barking dogs. Every dog in the street seemed to be barking—every kind of dog, not only the little ones but the big ones too. They were all facing East towards the way I was coming by. Then I turned round to look and had this vision, in Piccadilly, on the opposite side to the houses just after you pass the cab-rank.

---

[82] A main thoroughfare of London. By the time of Dunsany it was being converted from a place for pubs, booksellers and grand residences to more standard retail.

[83] This is from a real poem called *Hey Diddle Dinkety Poppety Pet* (yes you read that right) it goes:

Hey diddle dinkety poppety pet,

The merchants of London they wear scarlet,

Silk in the collar and gold in the hem,

So merrily march the merchant men.

Tall bent men were coming down the street arrayed in marvelous cloaks. All were sallow of skin and swarthy of hair, and most of them wore strange beards. They were coming slowly, and they walked with staves, and their hands were out for alms.

All the beggars had come to town.

I would have given them a gold doubloon engraven with the towers of Castile, but I had no such coin[84]. They did not seem the people to who it were fitting to offer the same coin as one tendered for the use of a taxicab (O marvelous, ill-made word, surely the pass-word some-where of some evil order)[85]. Some of them wore purple cloaks with wide green borders, and the border of green was a narrow strip with some, and some wore cloaks of old and faded red, and some wore violet cloaks, and none wore black. And they begged gracefully, as gods might beg for souls.

I stood by a lamp-post, and they came up to it, and one addressed it, calling the lamp-post brother, and said, "O lamp-post, our brother of the dark, are there many

---

[84] The "towers of castile" are the coat of arms of Castile and were incorporated into most later coats of arms of Spain, thus a fairly common image to find on Spanish doubloons.

[85] This was actually a new word at the time Dunsany was writing this. I think Dunsany rails against it because it's a compound of taxi-meter and cabriolet…and he seems to be the type of fellow who would rather say "taximeter cabriolet".

wrecks by thee in the tides of night? Sleep not, brother, sleep not. There were many wrecks an it were not for thee."

It was strange: I had not thought of the majesty of the street lamp and his long watching over drifting men. But he was not beneath the notice of these cloaked strangers.

And then one murmured to the street: "Art thou weary, street? Yet a little longer they shall go up and down, and keep thee clad with tar and wooden bricks. Be patient, street. In a while the earthquake cometh."

"Who are you?" people said. "And where do you come from?"

"Who may tell what we are," they answered, "or whence we come?"

And one turned towards the smoke-stained houses, saying, "Blessed be the houses, because men dream therein."

Then I perceived, what I had never thought, that all these staring houses were not alike, but different one from another, because they held different dreams.

And another turned to a tree that stood by the Green Park railings, saying, "Take comfort, tree, for the fields shall come again."

And all the while the ugly smoke went upwards, the smoke that has stifled Romance and blackened the birds. This, I thought, they can neither praise nor bless. And when they saw it they raised their hands towards it, towards the thousand chimneys, saying, "Behold the smoke. The old coal-forests that have lain so long in the dark, and so long still, are dancing now and going back to the sun. Forget not Earth, O our brother, and we wish thee joy of the sun."

It had rained, and a cheerless stream dropped down a dirty gutter. It had come from heaps of refuse, foul and forgotten; it had gathered upon its way things that were derelict, and went to somber drains unknown to man or the sun. It was this sullen stream as much as all other causes that had made me say in my heart that the town was vile, that Beauty was dead in it, and Romance fled.

Even this thing they blessed. And one that wore a purple cloak with broad green border, said, "Brother, be hopeful yet, for thou shalt surely come at last to the delectable Sea, and meet the heaving, huge, and travelled ships, and rejoice by isles that know the golden sun." Even thus they blessed the gutter, and I felt no whim to mock.

And the people that went by, in their black unseemly coats and their misshapen, monstrous, shiny hats, the beggars also blessed. And one of them said to one of these dark citizens: "O twin of Night himself, with thy specks of white at wrist and neck like to Night's scattered stars. How fearfully thou dost veil with black thy hid, unguessed desires. They are deep thoughts in thee that they will not frolic with colour, that they say 'No' to purple, and to lovely green 'Begone.' Thou hast wild fancies that they must needs be tamed with black, and terrible imaginings that they must be hidden thus. Has thy soul dreams of the angels, and of the walls of faëry that thou hast guarded it so utterly, lest it dazzle astonished eyes? Even so God hid the diamond deep down in miles of clay.

"The wonder of thee is not marred by mirth.

"Behold thou art very secret.

"Be wonderful. Be full of mystery."

Silently the man in the black frock-coat passed on. And I came to understand when the purple beggar had spoken, that the dark citizen had trafficked perhaps with Ind, that in his heart were strange and dumb ambitions; that his dumbness was founded by solemn rite on the roots of ancient tradition; that it might be overcome one day by a cheer in the street or by some one singing a song, and that when this shop-man spoke there might come clefts in the world and people peering over at the abyss.

Then turning towards Green Park, where as yet Spring was not, the beggars stretched out their hands, and looking at the frozen grass and the yet unbudding trees they, chanting all together, prophesied daffodils.

A motor omnibus came down the street, nearly running over some of the dogs that were barking ferociously still. It was sounding its horn noisily.

And the vision went then.

In a letter from a friend whom I have never seen, one of those that read my books, this line was quoted—"But he, he never came to Carcassonne." I do not know the origin of the line, but I made this tale about it.[86]

---

[86] This story is, to me, the seminal moment in this piece because it is Dunsany's story to himself. It is a reminder from Dunsany to Dunsany to not lose the wonder of the world, even as he saw it being transformed into an industrial grey. And thus it is the preface for perhaps his greatest story about not giving up on that wonder.

When Camorak reigned at Arn, and the world was fairer, he gave a festival to all the weald[88] to commemorate the splendour of his youth.

They say that his house at Arn was huge and high, and its ceiling painted blue; and when evening fell men would climb up by ladders and light the scores of candles hanging from slender chains. And they say, too, that sometimes a cloud would come, and pour in through the top of one of the oriel windows, and it would come over the edge of the stonework as the sea-mist comes over a sheer cliffs shaven lip where an old wind has blown for ever and ever (he has swept away thousands of leaves and thousands of centuries, they are all one to him, he owes no allegiance to Time). And the cloud would re-shape itself in the hall's lofty vault and drift on through it slowly, and out to the sky again through another window. And from its shape

---

[87] The Carcassonne in our world is a truly stunning castle-town in southern France. It looks like a place for medieval Romances and great quests. But Dunsany was probably inspired by well-known poem and folk song by Gustave Nadau about a man who longs to see, but never gets to, Carcassonne.

[88] As used in Poltarnees, Weald means woodland, though it is possibly used here because of how much it sounds like "world".

the knights in Camorak's hall would prophesy the battles and sieges of the next season of war. They say of the hall of Camorak at Arn that there hath been none like it in any land, and foretell that there will be never.

Hither had come in the folk of the Weald[89] from sheepfold and from forest, revolving slow thoughts of food, and shelter, and love, and they sat down wondering in that famous hall; and therein also were seated the men of Arn, the town that clustered round the King's high house, and all was roofed with red, maternal earth.

If old songs may be trusted, it was a marvelous hall.

Many who sat there could only have seen it distantly before, a clear shape in the landscape, but smaller than a hill. Now they beheld along the wall the weapons of Camorak's men, of which already the lute-players made songs, and tales were told at evening in the byres. There they described the shield of Camorak that had gone to and fro across so many battles, and the sharp but dinted edges of his sword; there were the weapons of Gadriol the Leal[90], and Norn, and Athoric of the Sleety Sword, Heriel the Wild, Yarold, and Thanga of Esk[91], their arms hung

---

[89] Amusingly, "Weald" when capitalized usually refers to a specific part of England.

[90] Faithful and honest.

[91] Dunsany's uses character names to help define the type of story that he's trying to deliver. The style and structure of these names help place this story in the tradition of Celtic myth and Romance.

evenly all round the hall, low where a man could reach them; and in the place of honour in the midst, between the arms of Camorak and of Gadriol the Leal, hung the harp of Arleon. And of all the weapons hanging on those walls none were more calamitous to Camorak's foes than was the harp of Arleon[92]. For to a man that goes up against a strong place on foot, pleasant indeed is the twang and jolt of some fearful engine of war that his fellow-warriors are working behind him, from which huge rocks go sighing over his head and plunge among his foes; and pleasant to a warrior in the wavering light are the swift commands of his King, and a joy to him are his comrades' instant cheers exulting suddenly at a turn of the war. All this and more was the harp to Camorak's men; for not only would it cheer his warriors on, but many a time would Arleon of the Harp strike wild amazement into opposing hosts by some rapturous prophecy suddenly shouted out while his hand swept over the roaring strings. Moreover, no war was ever declared till Camorak and his men had listened long to the harp, and were elate with the music and mad against peace. Once Arleon, for the sake of a rhyme, had made war upon Estabonn; and an evil king was overthrown, and honour and glory won; from such queer motives does good sometimes accrue.

---

[92] It's not by chance that Dunsany sets up the art and the storyteller to be stronger than the sword.

Above the shields and the harps all round the hall were the painted figures of heroes of fabulous famous songs. Too trivial, because too easily surpassed by Camorak's men, seemed all the victories that the earth had known; neither was any trophy displayed of Camorak's seventy battles, for these were as nothing to his warriors or him com-pared with those things that their youth had dreamed and which they mightily purposed yet to do[93].

Above the painted pictures there was darkness, for evening was closing in, and the candles swinging on their slender chain were not yet lit in the roof; it was as though a piece of the night had been builded into the edifice like a huge natural rock that juts into a house. And there sat all the warriors of Arn and the Weald-folk wondering at them; and none were more than thirty, and all were skilled in war. And Camorak sat at the head of all, exulting in his youth.

We must wrestle with Time for some seven decades, and he is a weak and puny antagonist in the first three bouts.

Now there was present at this feast a diviner, one who knew the schemes of Fate, and he sat among the people

---

[93] Dunsany is setting up not only how powerful this group of warri-ors is, but also how trivial all the exploits of the world, including their own, are compared to what they might yet do, leaving the reader to decide whether the quest that takes up the rest of this story is waste of potential or actually the greatest of all possible quests.

of the Weald and had no place of honour, for Camorak and his men had no fear of Fate. And when the meat was eaten and the bones cast aside, the king rose up from his chair, and having drunken wine, and being in the glory of his youth and with all his knights about him, called to the diviner, saying, "Prophesy."

And the diviner rose up, stroking his grey beard, and spake guardedly—"There are certain events," he said, "upon the ways of Fate that are veiled even from a diviner's eyes, and many more are clear to us that were better veiled from all; much I know that is better unforetold, and some things that I may not foretell on pain of centuries of punishment. But this I know and foretell—that you will never come to Carcassonne."

Instantly there was a buzz of talk telling of Carcassonne—some had heard of it in speech or song, some had read of it, and some had dreamed of it. And the king sent Arleon of the Harp down from his right hand to mingle with the Weald-folk to hear aught that any told of Carcassonne. But the warriors told of the places they had won to—many a hard-held fortress, many a far-off land, and swore that they would come to Carcassonne.

And in a while came Arleon back to the king's right hand, and raised his harp and chanted and told of Carcassonne. Far away it was, and far and far away, a city of gleaming ramparts rising one over other, and marble terraces behind the ramparts, and fountains shimmering on the terraces. To Carcassonne the elf-kings with their fairies had first retreated from men, and had built it on an evening late in May by blowing their elfin horns. Carcassonne! Carcassonne!

Travellers had seen it sometimes like a clear dream, with the sun glittering on its citadel upon a far-off hilltop, and then the clouds had come or a sudden mist; no one had seen it long or come quite close to it; though once there were some men that came very near, and the smoke from the houses blew into their faces, a sudden gust—no more, and these declared that some one was burning cedarwood there. Men had dreamed that there is a witch there, walking alone through the cold courts and corridors of marmorean[94] palaces, fearfully beautiful and still for all her fourscore centuries, singing the second oldest song, which was taught her by the sea, shedding tears for loneliness from eyes that would madden armies, yet will she not call her dragons home—Carcassonne is terribly guarded. Sometimes she swims in a marble bath through whose deeps a river tumbles, or lies all morning on the edge of it to dry slowly in the sun, and watches the heaving river trouble the deeps of the bath. It flows through the caverns of earth for further than she knows, and coming

---

[94] Marble-like.

to light in the witch's bath goes down through the earth again to its own peculiar sea.

In autumn sometimes it comes down black with snow that spring has molten in unimagined mountains, or withered blooms of mountain shrubs go beautifully by.

When there is blood in the bath she knows there is war in the mountains; and yet she knows not where those mountains are.

When she sings the fountains dance up from the dark earth, when she combs her hair they say there are storms at sea, when she is angry the wolves grow brave and all come down to the byres[95], when she is sad the sea is sad, and both are sad for ever. Carcassonne! Carcassonne![96]

This city is the fairest of the wonders of Morning; the sun shouts when he beholdeth it; for Carcassonne Evening weepeth when Evening passeth away.

And Arleon told how many goodly perils were round about the city, and how the way was unknown, and it was a knightly venture. Then all the warriors stood up and sang of the splendour of the venture. And Camorak swore by the gods that had builded Arn, and by the honour of his

---

[95] Cowsheds.

[96] The use of 'Carcassonne! Carcassonne!' here mirrors its use earlier as the sound the elfin horns make at the raising of Carcassonne (and appear to be a nod to the Gustave Nadaud poem in which every stanza ends with "Carcassonne!")

warriors that, alive or dead, he would come to Carcassonne.

But the diviner rose and passed out of the hall, brushing the crumbs from him with his hands and smoothing his robe as he went.

Then Camorak said, "There are many things to be planned, and counsels to be taken, and provender to be gathered. Upon what day shall we start?" And all the warriors answering shouted, "Now." And Camorak smiled thereat, for he had but tried them. Down then from the walls they took their weapons, Sikorix, Kelleron, Aslof, Wole of the Axe; Huhenoth, Peace-breaker; Wolwuf, Father of War; Tarion, Lurth of the Warcry and many another. Little then dreamed the spiders that sat in that ringing hall of the unmolested leisure they were soon to enjoy.

When they were armed they all formed up and marched out of the hall, and Arleon strode before them singing of Carcassonne.

But the talk of the Weald arose and went back well fed to byres. They had no need of wars or of rare perils. They were ever at war with hunger. A long drought or hard winter were to them pitched battles; if the wolves entered a sheep-fold it was like the loss of a fortress, a thunderstorm on the harvest was like an ambuscade. Well-fed, they went back slowly to their byres, being at truce with hunger; and the night filled with stars[97].

And black against the starry sky appeared the round helms of the warriors as they passed the tops of the ridges, but in the valleys they sparkled now and then as the starlight flashed on steel.

They followed behind Arleon going south, whence rumours had always come of Carcassonne: so they marched in the starlight, and he before them singing.

When they had marched so far that they heard no sound from Arn, and even inaudible were her swinging bells, when candles burning late far up in towers no longer sent them their disconsolate welcome; in the midst of the pleasant night that lulls the rural spaces, weariness came upon Arleon and his inspiration failed. It failed slowly. Gradually he grew less sure of the way to Carcassonne. Awhile he stopped to think, and remembered the way again; but his clear certainty was gone, and in its place were efforts in his mind to recall old prophecies and shepherd's songs that told of the marvelous city. Then as he said over carefully to himself a song that a wanderer had learnt from a goatherd's boy far up the lower slope of ultimate southern mountains, fatigue came down upon his toiling mind

---

[97] Dunsany's worry about an upcoming European war echo through all these stories, but here perhaps are his thoughts clearest.

like snow on the winding ways of a city noisy by night, stilling all[98].

He stood, and the warriors closed up to him. For long they had passed by great oaks standing solitary here and there, like giants taking huge breaths of the night air before doing some furious deed; now they had come to the verge of a black forest; the tree-trunks stood like those great columns in an Egyptian hall whence God in an older mood received the praise of men; the top of it sloped the way of an ancient wind. Here they all halted and lighted a fire of branches, striking sparks from flint into a heap of bracken. They eased them of their armour, and sat round the fire, and Camorak stood up there and addressed them, and Camorak said: "We go to war with Fate, who has doomed that I shall not come to Carcassonne. And if we turn aside but one of the dooms of Fate, then the whole future of the world is ours, and the future that Fate has ordered is like the dry course of an averted river. But if such men as we, such resolute conquerors, cannot prevent one doom that Fate has planned, then is the race of man enslaved for ever to do its petty and allotted task.[99]"

---

[98] Thoughts of aging and loss of creativity clearly weighed on Dunsany as he wrote Dreamers Tales, hence it becomes a recurring theme.

[99] This is perhaps the most important passage of Carcassonne. It is the reason that I find it so inspiring and the reason that their striving without end, even if the cause is hopeless, is so important.

Then they all drew their swords, and waved them high in the fire-light, and declared war on Fate.

Nothing in the somber forest stirred or made any sound.

Tired men do not dream of war. When morning came over the gleaming fields a company that had set out from Arn discovered the discovered the camping-place of the warriors, and brought pavilions and provender. And the warriors feasted, and the birds in the forest sang, and the inspiration of Arleon awoke.

Then they rose, and following Arleon, entered the forest, and marched away to the South. And many a woman of Arn sent her thoughts with them as they played alone some old monotonous tune, but their own thoughts were far before them, skimming over the bath through whose deeps the river tumbles in marble Carcassonne.

When butterflies were dancing on the air, and the sun neared the zenith, pavilions were pitched, and all the warriors rested; and then they feasted again, and then played knightly games, and late in the afternoon marched on once more, singing of Carcassonne.

And night came down with its mystery on the forest, and gave their demoniac look again to the trees, and rolled up out of misty hollows a huge and yellow moon.

And the men of Arn lit fires, and sudden shadows arose and leaped fantastically away. And the night-wind blew, arising like a ghost, and passed between the tree trunks, and slipped down shimmering glades, and waked the prowling beasts still dreaming of day, and drifted nocturnal birds afield to menace timorous things, and beat the roses of the befriending night, and wafted to the ears of wandering men the sound of a maiden's song, and gave a glamour to the lutanist's tune played in his loneliness on distant hills; and the deep eyes of moths glowed like a galleon's lamps, and they spread their wings and sailed their familiar sea. Upon this night-wind also the dreams of Camorak's men floated to Carcassonne.

All the next morning they marched, and all the evening, and knew they were nearing now the deeps of the forest. And the citizens of Arn kept close together and close behind the warriors. For the deeps of the forest were all unknown to travellers, but not unknown to those tales of fear that men tell at evening to their friends, in the comfort and the safety of their hearths. Then night appeared, and an enormous moon. And the men of Camorak slept. Sometimes they woke, and went to sleep again; and those that stayed awake for long and listened heard heavy two-footed creatures pad through the night on paws.

As soon as it was light the unarmed men of Arn began to slip away, and went back by bands through the forest. When darkness came they did not stop to sleep, but continued their flight straight on until they came to Arn, and added there by the tales they told to the terror of the forest.

But the warriors feasted, and afterwards Arleon rose, and played his harp, and led them on again; and a few faithful servants stayed with them still. And they marched all day through a gloom that was as old as night, but Arleon's inspiration burned in his mind like a star. And he led them till the birds began to drop into the treetops, and it was evening and they all encamped. They had only one pavilion left to them now, and near it they lit a fire, and Camorak posted a sentry with drawn sword just beyond the glow of the firelight. Some of the warriors slept in the pavilion and others round about it.

When dawn came something terrible had killed and eaten the sentry. But the splendour of the rumours of Carcassonne and Fate's decree that they should never come there, and the inspiration of Arleon and his harp, all urged the warriors on; and they marched deeper and deeper all day into the forest.

Once they saw a dragon that had caught a bear and was playing with it, letting it run a little way and overtaking it with a paw.

They came at last to a clear space in the forest just before nightfall. An odour of flowers arose from it like a mist, and every drop of dew interpreted heaven unto itself.

It was the hour when twilight kisses Earth.

It was the hour when a meaning comes into senseless things, and trees out-majesty the pomp of monarchs, and the timid creatures steal abroad to feed, and as yet the beasts of prey harmlessly dream, and Earth utters a sigh, and it is night.

In the midst of the wide clearing Camorak's warriors camped, and rejoiced to see stars again appearing one by one.

That night they ate the last of their provisions, and slept unmolested by the prowling things that haunt the gloom of the forest.

On the next day some of the warriors hunted stags, and others lay in rushes by a neighbouring lake and shot arrows at water-fowl. One stag was killed, and some geese, and several teal.

Here the adventurers stayed, breathing the pure wild air that cities know not; by day they hunted, and lit fires by night, and sang and feasted, and forgot Carcassonne. The terrible denizens of the gloom never molested them, venison was plentiful, and all manner of water-fowl: they loved the chase by day, and by night their favourite songs. Thus day after day went by, thus week after week. Time flung over this encampment a handful of moons, the gold and silver moons that waste the year away; Autumn and Winter passed, and Spring appeared; and still the warriors hunted and feasted there[100].

---

[100] Dunsany is using this to point out that while some fail to fight fate from fear (the servants from earlier) others abandon the struggle for ease.

One night of the springtide they were feasting about a fire and telling tales of the chase, and the soft moths came out of the dark and flaunted their colours in the firelight, and went out grey into the dark again; and the night wind was cool upon the warriors' necks, and the camp-fire was warm in their faces, and a silence had settled among them after some song, and Arleon all at once rose suddenly up, remembering Carcassonne. And his hand swept over the strings of his harp, awaking the deeper chords, like the sound of a nimble people dancing their steps on bronze, and the music rolled away into the night's own silence, and the voice of Arleon rose:

"When there is blood in the bath she knows there is war in the mountains and longs for the battle-shout of kingly men."

And suddenly all shouted, "Carcassonne!" And at that word their idleness was gone as a dream is gone from a dreamer waked with a shout. And soon the great march began that faltered no more nor wavered. Unchecked by battles, undaunted in lonesome spaces, ever unwearied by the vulturous years, the warriors of Camorak held on; and Arleon's inspiration led them still. They cleft with the music of Arleon's harp the gloom of ancient silences; they went singing into battles with terrible wild men, and came out singing, but with fewer voices; they came to villages in valleys full of the music of bells, or saw the lights at dusk of cottages sheltering others.

They became a proverb for wandering, and a legend arose of strange, disconsolate men. Folks spoke of them at nightfall when the fire was warm and rain slipped down the eaves; and when the wind was high small children feared the Men Who Would Not Rest were going clattering past. Strange tales were told of men in old grey armour moving at twilight along the tops of the hills and never asking shelter; and mothers told their boys who grew impatient of home that the grey wanderers were once so impatient and were now hopeless of rest, and were driven along with the rain whenever the wind was angry.

But the wanderers were cheered in their wandering by the hope of coming to Carcassonne, and later on by anger against Fate, and at last they marched on still because it seemed better to march on than to think.

For many years they had wandered and had fought with many tribes; often they gathered legends in villages and listened to idle singers singing songs; and all the rumours of Carcassonne still came from the South.

And then one day they came to a hilly land with a legend in it that only three valleys away a man might see, on clear days, Carcassonne. Tired though they were and few, and worn with the years which had all brought them wars, they pushed on instantly, led still by Arleon's inspiration which dwindled in his age, though he made music with his old harp still.

All day they climbed down into the first valley and for two days ascended, and came to the Town That May Not Be Taken In War below the top of the mountain, and its gates were shut against them, and there was no way round. To left and right steep precipices stood for as far as eye could see or legend tell of, and the pass lay through the city. Therefore Camorak drew up his remaining warriors in line of battle to wage their last war, and they stepped forward over the crisp bones of old, unburied armies.

No sentinel defied them in the gate, no arrow flew from any tower of war. One citizen climbed alone to the mountain's top, and the rest hid themselves in sheltered places.

Now, in the top of the mountain was a deep, bowl-like cavern in the rock, in which fires bubbled softly. But if any cast a boulder into the fires, as it was the custom for one of those citizens to do when enemies approached them, the mountain hurled up intermittent rocks for three days, and the rocks fell flaming all over the town and all round about it. And just as Camorak's men began to batter the gate they heard a crash on the mountain, and a great rock fell beyond them and rolled into the valley. The next two fell in front of them on the iron roofs of the town. Just as they entered the town a rock found them crowded in a narrow street, and shattered two of them[101]. The mountain smoked and panted; with every pant a rock plunged into the streets or bounced along the heavy iron roof, and the smoke went slowly up, and up, and up.

When they had come through the long town's empty streets to the locked gate at the end, only fifteen were left. When they had broken down the gate there were only ten alive. Three more were killed as they went up the slope, and two as they passed near the terrible cavern. Fate let the rest go some way down the mountain upon the other side, and then took three of them. Camorak and Arleon alone were left alive. And night came down on the valley to which they had come, and was lit by flashes from the fatal mountain; and the two mourned for their comrades all night long.

But when the morning came they remembered their war with Fate, and their old resolve to come to Carcassonne, and the voice of Arleon rose in a quavering song, and snatches of music from his old harp, and he stood up and marched with his face southwards as he had done for years, and behind him Camorak went. And when at last

---

[101] This is the ultimate frustration and the ultimate indignity. They are not fighting against anything. Their lives are not taken in battle against a great foe or opposing some terrible evil. Instead they're swept aside by chance, by fate. And yet it that makes it the truest battle in the tale, for it is against fate they fight and warrior by warrior they day rather that surrender that war.

they climbed from the third valley, and stood on the hill's summit in the golden sunlight of evening, their aged eyes saw only miles of forest and the birds going to roost.

Their beards were white, and they had travelled very far and hard; it was the time with them when a man rests from labours and dreams in light sleep of the years that were and not of the years to come.

Long they looked southwards; and the sun set over remoter forests, and glow-worms lit their lamps, and the inspiration of Arleon rose and flew away for ever, to gladden, perhaps, the dreams of younger men.

And Arleon said: "My King, I know no longer the way to Carcassonne."

And Camorak smiled, as the aged smile, with little cause for mirth, and said: "The years are going by us like huge birds, whom Doom and Destiny and the schemes of God have frightened up out of some old grey marsh. And it may well be that against these no warrior may avail, and that Fate has conquered us, and that our quest has failed."

And after this they were silent.

Then they drew their swords, and side by side went down into the forest, still seeking Carcassonne[102].

---

[102] This is why Dunsany matters to me. Because achievement of the quest is less important than what the quest stands for. Practicality takes second place to meaning.

I think they got not far; for there were deadly marshes in that forest, and gloom that outlasted the nights, and fearful beasts accustomed to its ways. Neither is there any legend, either in verse or among the songs of the people of the fields, of any having come to Carcassonne.

In Zaccarath¹⁰³

"Come," said the King in sacred Zaccarath, "and let our prophets prophesy before us."

A far-seen jewel of light was the holy palace, a wonder to the no-mads on the plains.

There was the King with all his underlords, and the lesser kings that did him vassalage, and there were all his queens with all their jewels upon them.

Who shall tell of the splendour in which they sat; of the thousand lights and the answering emeralds; of the dangerous beauty of that hoard of queens, or the flash of their laden necks?

There was a necklace there of rose-pink pearls beyond the art of the dreamer to imagine. Who shall tell of the amethyst chandeliers, where torches, soaked in rare Bhyrinian oils, burned and gave off a scent of blethany?

(This herb marvellous, which, growing near the summit of Mount Zaumnos, scents all the Zaumnian range, and is smelt far out on the Kepuscran plains, and even,

---

¹⁰³ Dunsany later said that this work was inspired by what he saw as blindness towards the inevitability of the first world war. This is easy to miss in the reading of it but seems incredibly likely when pointed out.

when the wind is from the mountains, in the streets of the city of Ognoth. At night it closes its petals and is heard to breathe, and its breath is a swift poison. This it does even by day if the snows are disturbed about it. No plant of this has ever been captured alive by a hunter.)

Enough to say that when the dawn came up it appeared by contrast pallid and unlovely and stripped bare of all its glory, so that it hid itself with rolling clouds.

"Come," said the King, "let our prophets prophesy."

Then the heralds stepped through the ranks of the King's silk-clad warriors who lay oiled and scented upon velvet cloaks, with a pleasant breeze among them caused by the fans of slaves; even their casting-spears were set with jewels; through their ranks the heralds went with mincing steps, and came to the prophets, clad in brown and black, and one of them they brought and set him before the King. And the King looked at him and said, "Prophesy unto us."

And the prophet lifted his head, so that his beard came clear from his brown cloak, and the fans of the slaves that fanned the warriors wafted the tip of it a little awry. And he spake to the King, and spake thus:

"Woe unto thee, King, and woe unto Zaccarath. Woe unto thee, and woe unto thy women, for your fall shall be sore and soon. Already in Heaven the gods shun thy god: they know his doom and what is written of him: he sees oblivion before him like a mist. Thou hast aroused the hate of the mountaineers. They hate thee all along the crags of Droom[104]. The evilness of thy days shall bring down the Zeedians on thee as the suns of springtide bring the avalanche down. They shall do unto Zaccarath as the avalanche doth unto the hamlets of the valley." When the queens chattered or tittered among themselves, he merely raised his voice and still spake on: "Woe to these walls and the carven things upon them. The hunter shall know the camping-places of the nomads by the marks of the camp-fires on the plain, but he shall not know the place of Zaccarath."

A few of the recumbent warriors turned their heads to glance at the prophet when he ceased. Far overhead the echoes of his voice hummed on awhile among the cedarn rafters.

"Is he not splendid?" said the King. And many of that assembly beat with their palms upon the polished floor in token of applause[105]. Then the prophet was conducted back to his place at the far end of that mighty hall, and for a while musicians played on marvellous curved horns, while drums throbbed behind them hidden in a recess.

---

[104] Always one to play with words here Dunsany give us something that sounds much like Mount Doom, and yet also means "the crags of Dream" if you take the Dutch meaning of this word.
[105] Here we have the tie in with the First World War: the repeated ignoring of warnings, people, especially heads of state, hearing only what they wanted to hear.

The musicians were sitting crosslegged on the floor, all blowing their huge horns in the brilliant torchlight, but as the drums throbbed louder in the dark they arose and moved slowly nearer to the King. Louder and louder drummed the drums in the dark, and nearer and nearer moved the men with the horns, so that their music should not be drowned by the drums before it reached the King.

A marvellous scene it was when the tempestuous horns were halted before the King, and the drums in the dark were like the thunder of God; and the queens were nodding their heads in time to the music, with their diadems flashing like heavens of falling stars; and the warriors lifted their heads and shook, as they lifted them, the plumes of those golden birds which hunters wait for by the Liddian lakes, in a whole lifetime killing scarcely six, to make the crests that the warriors wore when they feasted in Zaccarath. Then the King shouted and the warriors sang—almost they remembered then old battle-chants. And, as they sang, the sound of the drums dwindled, and the musicians walked away backwards, and the drumming became fainter and fainter as they walked, and altogether ceased, and they blew no more on their fantastic horns. Then the assemblage beat on the floor with their palms. And afterwards the queens besought the King to send for another prophet. And the heralds brought a singer, and placed him before the King; and the singer was a young man with a harp. And he swept the strings of it, and when there was silence he sang of the iniquity of the King. And he foretold the onrush of the Zeedians, and the fall and the forgetting of Zaccarath, and the coming again of the desert to its own, and the playing about of little lion cubs where the courts of the palace had stood.

"Of what is he singing?" said a queen to a queen.

"He is singing of everlasting Zaccarath."

As the singer ceased the assemblage beat listlessly on the floor, and the

King nodded to him, and he departed.

When all the prophets had prophesied to them and all the singers sung, that royal company arose and went to other chambers, leaving the hall of festival to the pale and lonely dawn. And alone were left the lion-headed gods that were carven out of the walls; silent they stood, and their rocky arms were folded. And shadows over their faces moved like curious thoughts as the torches flickered and the dull dawn crossed the fields. And the colours began to change in the chandeliers.

When the last lutanist fell asleep the birds began to sing.

Never was greater splendour or a more famous hall. When the queens went away through the curtained door with all their diadems, it was as though the stars should arise in their stations and troop together to the West at sunrise.

And only the other day I found a stone that had undoubtedly been a part of Zaccarath, it was three inches long and an inch broad; I saw the edge of it uncovered by the sand. I believe that only three other pieces have been found like it[106].

---

[106] With this ending it's hard not to think that Shelly's *Ozymandias*, which Dunsany would surely have read, didn't serve as part of the inspiration for this story.

The Field

When one has seen Spring's blossom fall in London, and Summer appear and ripen and decay, as it does early in cities, and one is in London still, then, at some moment or another, the country places lift their flowery heads and call to one with an urgent, masterful clearness, upland behind upland in the twilight like to some heavenly choir arising rank on rank to call a drunkard from his gambling-hell. No volume of traffic can drown the sound of it, no lure of London can weaken its appeal. Having heard it one's fancy is gone, and evermore departed, to some coloured pebble agleam in a rural brook, and all that London can offer is swept from one's mind like some suddenly smitten metropolitan Goliath.

The call is from afar both in leagues and years, for the hills that call one are the hills that were, and their voices are the voices of long ago, when the elf-kings still had horns.

I see them now, those hills of my infancy (for it is they that call), with their faces upturned to the purple twilight, and the faint diaphanous figures of the fairies peering out from under the bracken to see if evening is come. I do not see upon their regal summits those desirable mansions, and highly desirable residences, which have lately been built for gentlemen who would exchange customers for tenants[107].

When the hills called I used to go to them by road, riding a bicycle. If you go by train you miss the gradual approach, you do not cast off London like an old forgiven sin, nor pass by little villages on the way that must have some rumour of the hills; nor, wondering if they are still the same, come at last upon the edge of their far-spread robes, and so on to their feet, and see far off their holy, welcoming faces. In the train you see them suddenly round a curve, and there they all are sitting in the sun.

I imagine that as one penetrated out from some enormous forest of the tropics, the wild beasts would become fewer, the gloom would lighten, and the horror of the place would slowly lift. Yet as one emerges nearer to the edge of London, and nearer to the beautiful influence of the hills, the houses become uglier, the streets viler, the gloom deepens, the errors of civilization stand bare to the scorn of the fields.

Where ugliness reaches the height of its luxuriance, in the dense misery of the place, where one imagines the

---

[107] Dunsany is critiquing here the trend he saw in his lifetime of abandoning the old English economic system of local landowners for a much more consumer-based economy. Although he has a romantic view of it, he sees it as the move from a personal system to an impersonal one and much of his writing is colored by his struggle against it, especially as a major landholder himself.

builder saying, "Here I culminate. Let us give thanks to Satan," there is a bridge of yellow brick[108], and through it, as through some gate of filigree silver opening on fairy-land, one passes into the country.

To left and right, as far as one can see, stretches that monstrous city; before one are the fields like an old, old song.

There is a field there that is full of king-cups. A stream runs through it, and along the stream is a little wood of osiers[109]. There I used often to rest at the streams edge before my long journey to the hills.

There I used to forget London, street by street. Some-times I picked a bunch of king-cups to show them to the hills.

I often came there. At first I noticed nothing about the field except its beauty and its peacefulness.

---

[108] Though I can find no evidence one way or the other, I can't help but think that Dunsany might have been inspired by the *Wonderful Wizard of Oz* which was released a few years earlier. That said, the type of brick that was commonly used for bridge building around London at that time was yellow in hew because of peculiarities of the local clay, but soot had stained all the bridges in London a fairly uniform black. It's quite possible that there was a real bridge that Dunsany would get to on his rides once he'd left London that seemed resplendently yellow and that marked for him the beginning of the countryside (though today we'd probably only think of it as a rather greyish yellow to be honest).

[109] A type of willow.

But the second time that I came I thought there was something ominous about the field.

Down there among the king-cups by the little shallow stream I felt that something terrible might happen in just such a place.

I did not stay long there, because I thought that too much time spent in London had brought on these morbid fancies and I went on to the hills as fast as I could.

I stayed for some days in the country air, and when I came back I went to the field again to enjoy that peaceful spot before entering London. But there was still something ominous among the osiers.

A year elapsed before I went there again. I emerged from the shadow of London into the gleaming sun; the bright green grass and the king-cups were flaming in the light, and the little stream was singing a happy song. But the moment I stepped into the field my old uneasiness returned, and worse than before. It was as though the shadow was brooding there of some dreadful future thing and a year had brought it nearer.

I reasoned that the exertion of bicycling might be bad for one, and that the moment one rested this uneasiness might result.

A little later I came back past the field by night, and the song of the stream in the hush attracted me down to it. And there the fancy came to me that it would be a terribly cold place to be in the starlight, if for some reason one was hurt and could not get away.

I knew a man who was minutely acquainted with the past history of that locality, and him I asked if anything historical had ever happened in that field. When he pressed me for my reason in asking him this, I said that the field had seemed to me such a good place to hold a pageant in. But he said that nothing of any interest had ever occurred there, nothing at all.

So it was from the future that the field's terrible trouble came.

For three years off and on I made visits to the field, and every time more clearly it boded evil things, and my uneasiness grew more acute every time that I was lured to go and rest among the cool green grass under the beautiful osiers. Once to distract my thoughts I tried to gauge how fast the stream was trickling, but I found myself wondering if it flowed faster than blood.

I felt that it would be a terrible place to go mad in, one would hear voices.

At last I went to a poet whom I knew, and woke him from huge dreams, and put before him the whole case of the field. He had not been out of London all that year, and he promised to come with me and look at the field, and tell me what was going to happen there. It was late in July when we went. The pavement, the air, the houses and the dirt had been all baked dry by the summer, the weary traffic dragged on, and on, and on, and Sleep spreading her wings soared up and floated from London and went to walk beautifully in rural places.

When the poet saw the field he was delighted, the flowers were out in masses all along the stream, he went down to the little wood rejoicing. By the side of the stream he stood and seemed very sad. Once or twice he looked up and down it mournfully, then he bent and looked at the king-cups, first one and then another, very closely, and shaking his head.

For a long while he stood in silence, and all my old uneasiness returned, and my bodings for the future.

And then I said, "What manner of field is it?"

And he shook his head sorrowfully.

"It is a battlefield," he said[110].

---

[110] This ties in with Dunsany's overarching feeling about the inevitability of the First World War. It's not by chance that in this story the only people who can tell that something terrible is going to happen are writers and poets.

The Day of the Poll[111]

In the town by the sea it was the day of the poll, and
the poet regarded it sadly when he woke and saw the light
of it coming in at his window between two small curtains
of gauze. And the day of the poll was beautifully bright;
stray bird-songs came to the poet at the window; the air
was crisp and wintry, but it was the blaze of sunlight that
had deceived the birds. He heard the sound of the sea that
the moon led up the shore, dragging the months away
over the pebbles and shingles and piling them up with the
years where the worn-out centuries lay; he saw the majes-
tic downs stand facing mightily southwards; saw the
smoke of the town float up to their heavenly faces—column after column rose calmly into the morning as house
by house was waked by peering shafts of the sunlight and
lit its fires for the day; column by column went up toward
the serene downs' faces, and failed before they came there
and hung all white over houses; and every one in the town
was raving mad.

It was a strange thing that the poet did, for he hired
the largest motor in the town and covered it with all the

---

[111] This is one of Dunsany's rare satirical pieces.

flags he could find, and set out to save an intelligence. And he presently found a man whose face was hot, who shouted that the time was not far distant when a candidate, whom he named, would be returned at the head of the poll by a thumping majority. And by him the poet stopped and offered him a seat in the motor that was covered with flags. When the man saw the flags that were on the motor, and that it was the largest in the town, he got in. He said that his vote should be given for that fiscal system that had made us what we are, in order that the poor man's food should not be taxed to make the rich man richer. Or else it was that he would give his vote for that system of tariff reform which should unite us closer to our colonies with ties that should long endure, and give employment to all[112]. But it was not to the polling-booth that the motor went, it passed it and left the town and came by a small white winding road to the very top of the downs. There the poet dismissed the car and let that wondering voter on to the grass and seated himself on a rug. And for long the voter talked of those imperial traditions that our forefathers had made for us and which he should uphold with his vote, or else it was of a people oppressed by a feudal

---

[112] All of these were talking points of his day but to reinforce the satire the voter repeats them all in a very contradictory manner as if he were just literally shouting every talking point someone had told him.

system that was out of date and effete, and that should be ended or mended[113]. But the poet pointed out to him small, distant, wandering ships on the sunlit strip of sea, and the birds far down below them, and the houses below the birds, with the little columns of smoke that could not find the downs.

And at first the voter cried for his polling-booth like a child; but after a while he grew calmer, save when faint bursts of cheering came twittering up to the downs, when the voter would cry out bitterly against the misgovernment of the Radical party, or else it was—I forget what the poet told me—he extolled its splendid record.

"See," said the poet, "these ancient beautiful things, the downs and the old-time houses and the morning, and the grey sea in the sunlight going mumbling round the world. And this is the place they have chosen to go mad in!"

And standing there with all broad England behind him, rolling northward, down after down, and before him the glittering sea too far for the sound of the roar of it, there seemed to the voter to grow less important the questions that troubled the town. Yet he was still angry.

"Why did you bring me here?" he said again.

---

[113] As the previous note.

"Because I grew lonely," said the poet, "when all the town went mad."

Then he pointed out to the voter some old bent thorns, and showed him the way that a wind had blown for a million years, coming up at dawn from the sea; and he told him of the storms that visit the ships, and their names and whence they come, and the currents they drive afield, and the way that the swallows go. And he spoke of the down where they sat, when the summer came, and the flowers that were not yet, and the different butterflies, and about the bats and the swifts, and the thoughts in the heart of man. He spoke of the aged windmill that stood on the down, and of how to children it seemed a strange old man who was only dead by day. And as he spoke, and as the sea-wind blew on that high and lonely place, there began to slip away from the voter's mind meaningless phrases that had crowded it long—thumping majority—victory in the fight—terminological inexactitudes—and the smell of paraffin lamps dangling in heated schoolrooms, and quotations taken from ancient speeches because the words were long. They fell away, though slowly, and slowly the voter saw a wider world and the wonder of the sea. And the afternoon wore on, and the winter evening came, and the night fell, and all black grew the sea, and about the time that the stars come blinking out to look upon our littleness, the polling-booth closed in the town.

When they got back the turmoil was on the wane in the streets; night hid the glare of the posters; and the tide, finding the noise abated and being at the flow, told an old tale that he had learned in his youth about the deeps of the sea, the same which he had told to coastwise ships that brought it to Babylon by the way of Euphrates before the doom of Troy.

I blame my friend the poet, however lonely he was, for preventing this man from registering his vote (the duty of every citizen); but perhaps it matters less, as it was a foregone conclusion, because the losing candidate, either through poverty or sheer madness, had neglected to subscribe to a single football club[114].

---

[114] In landing his last bit of satire Dunsany goes out of his way to let the reader know that he is not anti-voting, just that the way he saw it being carried out around him seemed to him mad.

The Unhappy Body

"Why do you not dance with us and rejoice with us?" they said to a certain body. And then that body made the confession of its trouble. It said: "I am united with a fierce and violent soul, that is altogether tyrannous and will not let me rest, and he drags me away from the dances of my kin to make me toil at his detestable work; and he will not let me do the little things, that would give pleasure to the folk I love, but only cares to please posterity when he has done with me and left me to the worms; and all the while he makes absurd demands of affection from those that are near to me, and is too proud even to notice any less than he demands, so that those that should be kind to me all hate me.[115]" And the unhappy body burst into tears.

And they said: "No sensible body cares for its soul. A soul is a little thing, and should not rule a body. You should drink and smoke more till he ceases to trouble you." But the body only wept, and said, "Mine is a fearful soul. I have driven him away for a little while with drink. But he will soon come back. Oh, he will soon come back!"

---

[115] This is probably a little bit of self-critique on the part of Dunsany.

And the body went to bed hoping to rest, for it was drowsy with drink. But just as sleep was near it, it looked up, and there was its soul sitting on the windowsill, a misty blaze of light, and looking into the river.

"Come," said the tyrannous soul, "and look into the street."

"I have need of sleep," said the body.

"But the street is a beautiful thing," the soul said vehemently; "a hundred of the people are dreaming there."

"I am ill through want of rest," the body said.

"That does not matter," the soul said to it. "There are millions like you in the earth, and millions more to go there. The people's dreams are wandering afield; they pass the seas and mountains of faëry, threading the intricate passes led by their souls; they come to golden temples a-ring with a thousand bells; they pass up steep streets lit by paper lanterns, where the doors are green and small; they know their way to witches' chambers and castles of enchantment; they know the spell that brings them to the causeway along the ivory mountains—on one side looking downward they behold the fields of their youth and on the other lie the radiant plains of the future. Arise and write down what the people dream."

"What reward is there for me," said the body, "if I write down what you bid me?"

"There is no reward," said the soul.

"Then I shall sleep," said the body.

And the soul began to hum an idle song sung by a young man in a fabulous land as he passed a golden city (where fiery sentinels stood), and knew that his wife was within it, though as yet but a little child, and knew by prophecy that furious wars, not yet arisen in far and unknown mountains, should roll above him with their dust and thirst before he ever came to that city again—the young man sang it as he passed the gate, and was now dead with his wife a thousand years.

"I cannot sleep for that abominable song," the body cried to the soul.

"Then do as you are commanded," the soul replied. And wearily the body took a pen again. Then the soul spoke merrily as he looked through the window. "There is a mountain lifting sheer above London, part crystal and part myst. Thither the dreamers go when the sound of the traffic has fallen. At first they scarcely dream because of the roar of it, but before midnight it stops, and turns, and ebbs with all its wrecks. Then the dreamers arise and scale the shimmering mountain, and at its summit find the galleons of dream. Thence some sail East, some West, some into the Past and some into the Future, for the galleons sail over the years as well as over the spaces, but mostly they head for the Past and the olden harbours, for thither the sighs of men are mostly turned, and the dream-ships go before them, as the merchantmen before the continual trade-winds go down the African coast. I see the galleons even now raise anchor after anchor; the stars flash by them; they slip out of the night; their prows go gleaming into the twilight of memory, and night soon lies far off, a black cloud hanging low, and faintly spangled with stars, like the harbour and shore of some low-lying land seen afar with its harbour lights."

Dream after dream that soul related as he sat there by the window. He told of tropical forests seen by unhappy men who could not escape from London, and never would—forests made suddenly wondrous by the song of some passing bird flying to unknown eyries and singing an unknown song. He saw the old men lightly dancing to the tune of elfin pipes—beautiful dances with fantastic maidens—all night on moonlit imaginary mountains; he heard far off the music of glittering Springs; he saw the fairness of blossoms of apple and may thirty years fallen[116]; he heard old voices—old tears came glistening back; Romance sat cloaked and crowned upon southern hills, and the soul knew him.

One by one he told the dreams of all that slept in that street. Sometimes he stopped to revile the body because it worked badly and slowly. Its chill fingers wrote as fast as they could, but the soul cared not for that. And so the

---

[116] Another hint that this piece is self-reflective as Dunsany was 31 when this book was first published.

night wore on till the soul heard tinkling in Oriental skies far footfalls of the morning.

"See now," said the soul, "the dawn that the dreamers dread. The sails of light are paling on those unwreckable galleons; the mariners that steer them slip back into fable and myth; that other sea the traffic is turning now at its ebb, and is about to hide its pallid wrecks, and to come swinging back, with its tumult, at the flow. Already the sunlight flashes in the gulfs behind the east of the world; the gods have seen it from their palace of twilight that they built above the sunrise; they warm their hands at its glow as it streams through their gleaming arches, before it reaches the world; all the gods are there that have ever been, and all the gods that shall be; they sit there in the morning, chanting and praising Man."

"I am numb and very cold for want of sleep," said the body.

"You shall have centuries of sleep," said the soul, "but you must not sleep now, for I have seen deep meadows with purple flowers flaming tall and strange above the brilliant grass, and herds of pure white unicorns that gambol there for joy, and a river running by with a glittering galleon on it, all of gold, that goes from an unknown inland to an unknown isle of the sea to take a song from the King of Over-the-Hills to the Queen of Far-Away.

"I will sing that song to you, and you shall write it down."

"I have toiled for you for years," the body said. "Give me now but one night's rest, for I am exceeding weary."

"Oh, go and rest. I am tired of you. I am off," said the soul.

And he arose and went, we know not whither. But the body they laid in the earth. And the next night at midnight the wraiths of the dead came drifting from their tombs to felicitate that body.

"You are free here, you know," they said to their new companion.

"Now I can rest," said the body[117].

---

[117] And thus *A Dreamer's Tales* ends...